# Impulse Spy

A Sonic Sleuths Series Mystery

## Carrie Ann Knox

# ONE

I first heard rather than saw her.

It was something in the sound of her boots that caught my attention. Or maybe the confident swish as she sashayed past my table. Whatever it was, I found myself abandoning the book in my hands to eye the mysterious girl.

I was clearly not the only one in the sleepy café to take notice. Yet as she strolled to the front counter, she seemed entirely unaware of any attention. A well-learned skill of the beautiful and striking, surely.

What was it about her, exactly? On paper, she didn't look all that different from me.

We both had long dark hair, although hers was a bit darker, almost black. While she was only a little taller, the combination of tight jeans under impossibly-high heeled black boots made her legs seem much longer than mine ever had. My blue eyes were bigger; hers had a narrowed, piercing look accentuated by the dark eyeliner that ringed them. I figured she was in her late twenties, like myself, but she somehow imparted an air of maturity and sophistication I rarely felt. I was intrigued by this sexier and more-refined doppelgänger.

It took the fumbling teenaged barista multiple tries to prepare her espresso and caramel macchiato. When proudly presented with the first tiny cup, she threw her head back and swallowed it in one gulp. She then grabbed the larger lidded coffee and strolled out the way she came, leaving behind a parting wink that set the young man's face on fire.

I returned my attention to the novel in my hands and the mundanity that was my day, eventually able to shake the image of the unfairly beautiful stranger. But the remainder of the bland bestselling so-called-thriller was now utterly uninspiring. I polished off my skinny latte and headed into the adjoining bookstore, intent on picking out my next read. I would need some vicarious excitement to get through the week.

But on the way to the mystery aisle, I became distracted. I spotted the girl again.

Coffee in hand, she was poring over a large reference manual of some kind while she spoke on her phone. I tried to continue on my way. Really, I did. But the language I heard wasn't English. It was deep and fast, vaguely eastern European. My best guess was Russian—a tongue quite unusual for our area of coastal Virginia. *Interesting.*

2

I hung a quick left into the cookbook section.

I found myself half-heartedly browsing the books on Italian and Mediterranean cuisine in front of me. Waiting. *For what?* I had no idea. I simply kept an eye on her. Inconspicuously, of course.

The girl finished her suspicious phone call and wandered away, oblivious. I waited until she settled in the spirituality section before I made my move. Ever so casually, I drifted over to her abandoned manual to check the contents. *What was the mysterious Russian-speaking girl up to?*

It was a dry tome on stock market trading. *She's a banker?* I flipped through, excitement fading. *Not exactly the femme fatale image I had going.*

I checked her position just as she replaced another large book and moved away again, this time out of sight. *Nothing to see here . . . but no harm in checking for sure, right?* I strolled to the vacated aisle, allowing myself one final act of intrusiveness.

The book she had been browsing was on occultism. *Intriguing.* I picked it up and leafed through. *Is she a witch? Maybe that explains my fascination.*

The sound of a voice being cleared startled me.

"Into the occult, are you?"

I looked up and found myself face to face with the object of my stalking. It occurred to me that the lilt of her voice sounded strictly American, no accent.

"Er, not really. I was just . . . curious." I looked down at the book sheepishly.

"Curious, huh?" Her cool eyes bore into me. "About the subject? Or about me?"

I replaced the book to avoid answering right away, my face reddening with embarrassment.

"I think I have my answer," she continued, a smile creeping onto her face. "You were following me. Why?"

I tried to come up with a reasonable explanation, but I was not sure myself. Why *was* I following this stranger?

"I don't know . . . boredom, I guess?"

She narrowed her eyes, dubious. "Boredom."

I shrugged. "I was going to find a new mystery to read. I guess I...wanted to check out a real-life mystery instead." I felt utterly foolish even saying it, but it was the only thing I could come up with.

Her mouth turned up on one side; she was laughing at me. "And I was a mystery?"

"I don't know, I . . . " I needed to get out of there as quickly as possible. "Seriously, I was just bored."

"Okay." She looked me over, sizing me up. "Well, I'd be happy to solve a mystery for you, but I wouldn't want to ruin any fun."

She was teasing me. *How do I get out of this?*

"How about this," she offered, leaning in conspiratorially. Her face turned intense, the words emphatic. "Do you want to know if I'm a *witch*?"

I hesitated, fairly certain she was messing with me. But I had to admit some lingering curiosity. And I saw no other way out. "Sure," I finally responded.

4

She laughed and shook her head, smiling. "No. I'm a writer. I come here sometimes to do research. Look things up."

"Oh," I replied stupidly, unable to think of anything else.

"The library has a lot more books," she continued, "but it's so quiet and there's no coffee." Her nose wrinkled. "Not really my scene."

I continued my impressive display of conversational skills. "Oh." I added a nod this time.

The girl studied me for another moment. "Well, I'd better get going." She smirked. "But be careful who you follow. Never know who you might stumble across by accident. Dangerous people out there."

"Right." I was sure my embarrassment was written all over my face.

The girl threw me a quick wink. "Later, Nancy Drew." She tossed her thick, shiny hair over her shoulder and strolled toward the entrance.

I shook my head at myself, appalled at my strange behavior. *Has to be all those books getting into my head.* I was officially banned from mysteries and thrillers for a while.

*** 

The vow didn't last very long. After a long workweek devoid of any pleasure reading, I was desperate for my fix. I would never make it through the weekend without a little suspense to spice things up. And that certainly wasn't going to come from my personal life at the moment.

Unfortunately, that would mean returning to the scene of humiliation. My safe little indie bookstore felt spoiled now. Epilogue Books had become my haven in this new town of Norfolk, VA. And I refused to find a new shop.

I would have to suck it up. *Just mind your own business this time.*

I strolled into the bookstore after work on Friday, head held high with faked indifference. The familiar smell of fresh-roasted beans from the café greeted me warmly. A quick circuit through the place assured me the maybe-not-so-mysterious girl was nowhere to be seen.

I sighed in relief and began to wander the fiction area, slowly feeling like myself again. An armful of books in hand, I eventually retired to the café and used them to reserve a quiet table in the corner while I purchased coffee.

When I returned with my latte, I found my eyes locked with an olive-skinned young man two tables away. He was staring blankly at me. I half-smiled politely as I sat down, but the young man held my gaze until I looked away and picked up the first book. *Curious.*

Detective novels were my favorite escape, and I had found a few newcomers. I planned to read a little of each to gauge my interest. The first didn't hook me right away, so I started a reject pile and picked up another. But as I sat back with the next option, I glanced up—and met the stranger's eyes yet again. No emotion or reaction, just staring from under thick black eyebrows. Unfalteringly.

I began to get just a shade unnerved. I sipped my coffee and tried to ignore the scrutiny. I worked to suppress my squirm reflex under his gaze.

Eventually I became engrossed enough in the story to tune out the attention. Having successfully found a winner, I reached for the final option in the stack—and a slip of paper floated to the floor.

I glanced up before bending to retrieve it. The young man was gone.

The scrap was simple stationary with a handwritten note:

*It was funny how I could feel all alone and under surveillance at the same time.*

Tiny hairs stood up on the back of my neck. I glanced around, paranoia creeping in. No one looking.

Trying to remain calm, I turned my attention back to the note and studied the neat script. The words were simple but seemed vaguely familiar. I pulled out my phone and did a quick search. The line was a quote from a young adult novel I had read. *Homeland.* I considered the meaning of the words.

*Surveillance?* Perhaps it was just a coincidence, a random scribbling left in the book by a fellow reader. This was a bookstore, after all. But the subject of the note

7

made me apprehensive. Especially given the young man's stare only moments before. And I didn't believe the paper had fallen out of the book. After double-checking—nothing inside—I decided to have a look at the origin of the quote to jog my memory.

Back in the fiction section, I searched for the author, Cory Doctorow. One copy of the novel on the shelf. I picked it up and thumbed through, trying to remember what the book was about. It was a sequel, about a paranoid tech-savvy teenager that uses technology to fight for privacy. Everyone in the novel was constantly under surveillance. As I flipped through, my eyes caught on a single line boldly underlined in pencil.

It was the same sentence that was left on the table for me to find. *This could not be a coincidence.*

I hustled back to my table with the book and started at the beginning. Upon closer inspection, I found more markings, but these were more faint. There were eight words lightly underlined in the book. I jotted down each word as I found it, and they quickly formed a sentence. *The spy who came in from the cold.*

I didn't need to look this one up. It was the title of one of the most famous spy novels of all time. Another spying reference. *Could someone be sending me a message?*

No, that would be crazy. *Right?* I tried to come up with a reasonable explanation. Could be just a coincidence. A hoax. Or maybe some kind of weird secret admirer thing?

Either way, I couldn't walk away just yet. There could be more. I went to fetch the John le Carre novel.

Once again, there was only one copy. My hands were a little shaky as I flipped through, page by page, looking for another message. There were no markings this time. *Darn.*

*Darn?*

*Well, it was fun while it lasted.*

But as I closed the book, something peeked out from behind the slipcover. A receipt. It was for coffee and a slice of pie, at a place called Joe's Diner. Never heard of it. It was dated two days prior, paid in cash.

I checked the book over once more. Nothing else was amiss. *Was this another clue? To what? Or was I losing my mind?* I checked to see if anyone was watching me. Again, no observers in sight.

I took the results of my bizarre scavenger hunt to the front to pay and hurried out, abandoning the books I had previously chosen. I wouldn't need a novel to keep me occupied tonight.

# TWO

I'd intended to go straight home.

Instead I found myself sitting outside Joe's Diner, watching through the windows. The curiosity was too strong to ignore.

It had begun to drizzle since I left the bookstore. The place was a small old-fashioned diner in a grittier section of town I was not familiar with. The weed-eaten parking lot was mostly empty. I watched the bored-looking waitresses and decided the place seemed non-threatening enough.

I entered and took a worn vinyl booth in the back. A middle-aged waitress perked up and hustled over. Her nametag read "Dottie."

"Evenin'. What can I get ya?"

"I'll take a coffee. Decaf." I fished out the receipt. "And can I ask you about something?"

"Do my best," she answered.

I handed her the receipt. "Is there any way to know who this receipt belongs to? I need to speak to them."

The woman studied the slip and shook her head.

"Sorry darlin'. But they paid in cash, and we don't exactly have a camera system here. Don't see any way to tell."

"Would anyone remember who came in?"

Dottie chuckled, a wheezing smoker's laugh that sounded more like a cough. "Orderin' coffee and pie ain't exactly unusual around here. That's what we're known for." She handed the receipt back to me. "Best pie in town," she added.

"Ok, thanks anyway." As she walked away, I called after her. "Go ahead and bring me a piece of pie, too. Whatever's most popular."

"You got it, honey." She hurried back behind the counter.

I stared at the receipt again, trying to come up with an explanation for everything. *Why was I brought here?* Perhaps the receipt was not a message at all. It could've been left in the book by anyone. But I refused to believe that everything was a coincidence.

I watched the handful of other patrons, almost all men in smudged work gear. Most were alone, reading the newspaper or staring out the windows as they ate. I figured they were on a break from one of the nearby industrial sites.

My mind in knots, I finally gave up and tried to relax as I nibbled on my crumbly apple pie. It really was quite good. I enjoyed sound of the rain outside, which had picked up as the sky turned dark. The ceiling fans lazily stirring the fresh coffee aroma were hypnotic.

I liked this place, a vestige of a long-lost era. Still confused but contented, I finished my pie and told myself I would come back another day.

I didn't realize at the time that someone else would make sure of that.

*** 

With the puzzling trail of clues gone cold, I was back to the usual grind as a fourth-year audiology fellow itching for graduation. A few months and a research project were all that stood in my way. To that end, my adviser had requested I attend a lecture by a visiting researcher after work and report back.

My boss, Dr. Seymore, had invited herself to join me. *No added pressure.* To avoid adding an awkward commute to the event with my boss, I snuck out of work as quickly as possible and hustled to the light-rail trail station. It would be my first ride.

The tiny train reminded me of an amusement-park monorail, and the crowd was boisterous. But by the second stop most of the passengers had cleared, leaving only two others on board my car. And that's when I noticed him looking at me.

The twenty-something Asian man struck a casual pose as he stared, kicked back with his leg across the adjacent seat. He had side-swept fringe and an eclectically-layered outfit; definitely a hacker vibe. His eyes didn't shift when I returned the gaze. He didn't even flinch. *Oh no—not this again.*

I tried to hide my discomfort by returning my attention out the window. But I could feel his eyes on me. I'm pretty sure he was smiling subtly, but it didn't feel lewd. It felt intentionally disturbing.

The short ride remaining felt interminable. I tried slow-breathing techniques from past yoga classes to stay calm. Finally we pulled to a stop. I stifled a sigh of relief and headed for the door. But just as I neared the stranger, he leapt to his feet and faced me, blocking my way.

In a panic, I met the man's eyes. He was still just smiling.

"Excuse me," I mumbled with as much courage as I could muster.

He stared back intensely for a moment before speaking. "Eight p.m. Sharp."

"I'm sorry?"

His smile became a wide grin. Then without a word, he stepped to the side, freeing my path. I was able to scramble out the door just before it closed.

***

I was a mess when I arrived at the lecture hall. After making the remaining walk in record time with one eye over my shoulder, I was relieved to be back in a crowd. I rushed to take a seat amongst the other medical professionals and tried to calm my breathing. *What had just happened?*

"Good to see you, Quinn. Mind if I join you?"

I looked up to see Dr. Seymore hovering above me. I couldn't think straight yet but believed I had regained my composure. I forced my best smile.

"Of course," I replied, shifting to let her pass.

She took the seat next to me and pulled out a portfolio with a legal pad. Then she turned her attention back to me.

"I'm so glad you could attend tonight," she said. "It always impresses me when our students take the initiative and participate in activities that aren't required." She turned to give me a direct look. "The kind of thing I admire in the students we sometimes keep on as staff after graduation."

*Oh man, I would kill to be offered a position.* "Well, I can't take credit for the idea," I said. "My dissertation advisor recommended this talk. I think the research may relate to my study. A comparison of hearing protection devices in an industrial environment."

She smoothed her short brown hair as she looked at me amiably. "And how is your study coming along?"

I was so not in the mood for professional small talk. Actually, I wasn't in the right mindset for any sort of lecture either, but at least I wouldn't have to participate.

"All set to go," I said. "I have a local manufacturing facility lined up to participate, and approval from my dissertation committee. I'll begin gathering data in a couple of weeks."

"Good. Keep me apprised of your progress."

I nodded in answer. A moment later I pulled my own small notebook and pen out of my bag and readied it in my lap, hoping the presentation would cut off our chat shortly. Thankfully, the room did begin to quieten as the host moved to the podium. I felt myself relax a little when the lights dimmed. I could be alone with my thoughts again.

I tried to focus on the research. I really did. It was important for me in myriad ways. Unfortunately, I didn't hear a thing that was being said.

I immediately began to replay the train incident in my head over and over, trying to make sense of it. *It could've just been a crazy person.* I might have believed that before last week. But some strange things had happened since then.

Given that the last bizarre event also involved a staring stranger, I pondered the possibility that this one was delivering yet another message. *A secret message—who am I?* I felt unhinged even considering it.

I reached into my bag and discreetly removed the receipt for coffee and pie I had placed for safekeeping. I studied it quickly in my lap, then returned my eyes to the speaker to look engaged. Meanwhile, my mind was whirling.

*Is this the second part of the message?* He gave me a time. Maybe the receipt was the place. And I was supposed to go to the diner. At eight p.m. sharp. Tonight?

It seemed plausible, if anything did.

I would have to at least check it out, as farfetched as it seemed. If I hurried, I could probably get my car and make it there by eight o'clock after the lecture. But the idea of just showing up, without any idea of what I was walking into, made me uneasy. Was it still some secret admirer? *More likely a serial killer.*

No, I would prefer to scope the situation out ahead of time. Then I could abandon the plan if anything looked questionable. But I had to know. I couldn't possibly not know.

I also couldn't waste any more time at this lecture. All I could think about was figuring out the mystery. *My boss is going to be disappointed.* But I had to take my chances.

I would have to fake an illness and hope for the best. I had never been so devious before.

I began my ruse by holding my hand to my stomach. After a moment I drew a sharp breath and squeezed as if in pain. Then my other hand moved to my mouth and lingered while I breathed slowly. I ended the show with a quiet gagging emphasized by a slight jerk of my shoulders. I removed my hand and turned to Dr. Seymore, a pained and apologetic look on my face.

"I'm sorry. I'm not feeling well," I whispered. "I have to go."

She nodded in sympathy. I grabbed my bag and hustled out of the auditorium. I took a deep breath when I exited the building, mentally wrapping my head around the deception I had just committed. And the enigmatic situation I was about to throw myself into.

I truly didn't recognize myself.

# THREE

It was just getting dark when I neared the diner. I pulled my car into the lot of the mini-grocery next door, giving me a perfect view of the diner entrance. My car was well-camouflaged by the surrounding cars. I was pleased with my cunning. *All that mystery reading is paying off.*

I turned off the engine and cracked the window for a little air. The diner was again quiet, with only a handful of cars in the lot. No shady characters lingering. No creepy staring men so far.

I watched and waited, anxiously checking the time on my phone at regular intervals. Barely anything moved.

With ten minutes to the designated time, I finally spotted movement. A woman was approaching by foot. She was wearing a stylish black trench-style jacket, dark jeans and heels. Her dark hair was pulled back in a long ponytail. I couldn't make out her face at this distance and wished I had some sort of binoculars.

She headed down the front sidewalk toward the entrance. But just outside the door, she stopped and perched her leather shoulder bag on the dome of a large trash receptacle. She began digging through the bag as though searching for something. But while her hand was busy, her head tilted up slightly and rotated, as though she were scanning the surroundings instead.

Suspicion tingled the back of my neck. In a flash of inspiration, I grabbed my phone and snapped a picture, allowing me to zoom in on the distant figure in the photo. Her face was now clearly recognizable.

It was the girl from the bookstore.

*I knew it.* Deep down, a part of me had suspected she could be behind this all along. But I still had no idea what *this* was.

I continued watching closely through the zoomed camera, now filming. The girl stopped pretending to search her bag and extended an arm carefully into the opening and to the side, as though accessing the void surrounding the actual trashcan.

Her hand reappeared with a manila envelope. She quickly stuffed the envelope into her bag. With a final glance around her, she threw her bag back over her shoulder and continued on into the diner.

A hidden envelope. *What have I gotten myself into?*

My mind starting piecing together everything I knew so far. A mysterious stranger caught me snooping. And has brought me on some kind of weird chase, using clues that revolve around allusions to spying. And now she is clearly collecting the fruits of espionage.

Obviously she is a spy of some sort. I thought back to old movies. The spies are generally spying on a foreign country—and I saw her speaking Russian! *Maybe I've been following the instructions of a KGB agent.*

No, no, no. Surely that was implausible. Run-ins with spies aren't something that happens in normal life.

*What about all the shipyards and huge Navy presence here?* Maybe it's not so crazy.

*I'm outta here.* I was reaching for my seatbelt when a knock on my window made me jump.

I looked up to see the trench-coat-wearing witch-slash-Russian-spy. "Fancy seeing you here," she said, grinning widely.

I tried to maintain my composure as my pulse began to race. I stared back at her, unable to come up with a response.

Her brow furrowed. "You okay?"

*Don't let on!* "I'm fine."

She smiled again. "Then want to join me for a coffee?"

"Oh, sorry," I replied. "I have to get going."

Her face fell. "Oh." She glanced back at the diner for a moment, and then returned her gaze to me. "Then could I get a quick ride?"

All I wanted was to get out of there. "I'm really kind of in a hurry."

"It's not far, only a few blocks," she said. "I'd rather not walk back in the dark. I left my car."

I paused only momentarily, but she took it as a sign. In a blink she was at the passenger's side, waiting for me to unlock the door. I couldn't exactly speed off now without raising suspicion. I had no choice. I let her in and put the car in reverse.

After pointing me to the left out of the lot, the mysterious stranger broke the silence. "I thought you were coming to meet me. You made it this far."

"I was meeting . . . someone," I said reluctantly. "But I changed my mind."

She turned to face me. "Why?"

"Look, I just want to stay out of it," I said.

"Out of what?"

"I don't know. I don't know anything—and I don't want to know anything—about whatever it is you're into." Nervous, I began to ramble. "I promise I won't pay any more attention to you and I won't tell anyone. You don't need to worry about me. I just want to stay out of it."

Her eyes widened in surprise. Then she smiled as she processed my words. "Well now I'm dying to know. What is it you think I'm into?"

"I don't know. I mean you obviously . . . gather information." I needed to tread very carefully here.

"Yes, okay. And?"

I considered my words. "And . . . I'm not sure it's for a book. So it's probably for someone else. But I don't know who it is for, and I don't want to know."

"Oh, I get it. You think I'm some kind of spy? For someone questionable, maybe." Her grin was sly. "Nefarious even."

*Oh, crap.* I have to get out of this conversation. "It's none of my business. I just want to go on my way. Really."

She motioned for me to take a left turn.

I complied and continued. "I'm sorry I followed you, and I'm sorry I followed your clues. I'll keep my nose to myself from now on." *And I really regret the video of you on my phone.*

Her brow furrowed. "But I don't want you to. That's the whole point."

*I don't like where this is headed.* "Listen, I don't judge," I stammered. "I'm sure you have your reasons for whatever you do. But I'm American."

I quickly realized what I had let slip and scrambled to abort. "We should just stop talking about it now. I really need to get home."

She smiled over at me, quizzical. "American?"

I gulped.

She looked genuinely confused. "So you're concerned I'm not American? First, what makes you think that?"

"Err, well, you . . . speak other languages." *What have I done?*

"Yes, one. I really only use it with my father." She paused, considering. Suddenly her face lit up. "Ohhh, I get it. You think I'm a spy . . . for Russia? What, like in the KGB?" Her laugh bordered on hysterical.

*She thinks this is funny?* Do I have it all wrong, or is this exactly how a real spy would deny it? I cringed in confusion.

She seemed to notice my discomfort and turned serious. "No, it's not funny. I get that. I'm not laughing at you." She smiled broadly. "Well, maybe a little. But seriously, I'm not a Russian spy."

"Okay, I believe you." I nodded my head in reassurance.

She glanced over questioningly.

"Really. I just want to go home." I was confused and possibly embarrassed.

"Okay. We're here anyway. You can pull in up there." She pointed to a small parking lot fronting an ancient two-story office building on the right. A dark Nissan Z was the sole occupant of the lot.

I pulled up next to it and stopped the car.

"But I need you to know something first," she continued. "I *am* a spy of sorts. I obviously wasn't trying to hide that from you. I wanted to get your interest."

I opened my mouth to stop her again, but she continued.

"I spy privately, for whoever needs information. Mostly businesses, sometimes individuals. Suspicious lovers—although I try to stay away from those cases if I can help it."

I pondered this for a moment. "You mean like a Private Investigator? You're a PI?"

"Exactly like a PI," she said. "Only I don't call myself that. I prefer the term 'consultant.'"

"Consultant?"

She smiled. "I look into situations for people, find information, and then I 'consult' with them on the truth."

I studied her, dubious.

She shrugged. "Companies are always hiring consultants. Who knows what some of them actually do. A lot of the time probably nothing. But they're hired as a normal business expense, and no one ever questions it." She unzipped her bag and reached inside. "So it's just easier to hide my services under the label 'consulting.' But essentially, yes, I'm spying for them."

A private spy? This actually sounded plausible.

She handed me a business card. The name on the card read S. McKenzie, Consultant. There was a cute little symbol of an owl at the top. It looked real enough.

She gave me a direct look. "And I was hoping you'd consider helping me."

My eyes narrowed. "What kind of help?"

"Assisting with my investigations. I've been thinking about getting a partner, someone to help out here and there. And you just came along and practically begged for the job without even knowing it."

I felt my face redden. I *had* been acting strangely.

She continued. "And I like you, I think we could have fun. Besides, you have this whole wide-eyed innocent look about you. People would trust you. Sometimes the job calls for that, and I don't pull it off as well. I think we could make a great team."

It was starting to make sense now. "So you were, what, testing me?"

"Essentially, yes. I made a trail for you to follow. I saw you obviously had some interest in surveillance. So I left you some mysterious tidbits to see if you would be compelled to follow." She grinned at me. "You passed with flying colors. I hear you even asked about tracking the receipt. I'm impressed."

I felt a little pride at her words.

"You also showed up early to our meeting to check things out, which is smart," she continued. "But I'm afraid you saw something that gives the wrong impression. I didn't realize the conclusion you would come to, but it makes sense."

My cheeks flamed hotter. "Yeah, I thought I was going to be tried for treason."

She laughed. "I assure you I'm not doing this for the love of my country, any country." She shook her head and looked at me. "I serve a far greater purpose—cold, hard cash. Done right, it pays pretty well. And for the fun. What other job uses secrets as a currency?"

I looked back at her, considering. I remembered our previous conversation. "I thought you told me you were a writer."

"That's just my favorite cover. You can get away with almost anything if people think you're doing research." She shrugged. "Make it seem like you find them utterly fascinating, and most people will spill all their secrets. Everyone wants to be special."

Interesting tip. I made a mental note to watch out for overeager interest from this girl.

"I had no reason to lie to you, it's just habit," she continued. "I was checking out financial investment books, for a job. The witchcraft thing was just to see if you were following me."

I hung my head a little. *I must've been pretty obvious.*

She resumed her pitch. "My *job* is to listen in on people and watch them when they think no one is watching. And sometimes pretend to be someone else. You know you're intrigued. You could do it with me."

"I have a job," I responded carefully.

"I know," she said. "You could help me at night or on weekends. It could be a hobby. Investigating is not exactly a nine to five gig."

I studied her face as she gazed back expectantly. Suddenly a thought seemed to occur to her.

"How about a trial run?" she said. "You could come with me on an operation. Just watch if you want."

My eyes widened. "An operation?"

"Just a simple surveillance for now."

I needed some time to process all this. "I don't know."

"Just think about it. If you want to see what I do, to get a taste, meet me at Corridors downtown tomorrow night. Seven o'clock. No pressure."

I smiled warily as she opened the car door. "I'll think about it."

27

She grinned back. "Sure. Night." She hopped in the sports car and roared out of the lot. I watched the taillights recede in the distance.

*Surely I'm not really considering this.*

# FOUR

I hesitated on the sidewalk when I arrived outside the upscale downtown restaurant at exactly 6pm. *What in the world am I doing here?* Meeting a mysterious stranger to discuss spying was quite out of my comfort zone. My typical Saturday nights have recently revolved around takeout and the sofa. *I don't even know the girl's first name.*

But something had brought me this far. I couldn't go home without knowing more.

I checked my reflection in the front windows. My knee-length black skirt and buttoned gray cardigan looked plenty appropriate. I took a deep breath and headed inside.

The girl smiled broadly as she watched me approach her table. "I knew you'd show up."

"That makes one of us," I mumbled, slipping into an adjacent seat.

She extended her hand. "I'm Sloan. Sloan McKenzie."

"Quinn Bailey." I returned the offer.

"I know," she replied, flippant. "But it's nice to finally meet you."

I looked her over as my stomach clenched warily. I was pleased to see she was dressed similarly, her red cardigan dressed up further with a strand of delicate pearls. But the conservative look, dowdy on me, somehow imparted only class on her.

"So tell me, Quinn, what do you want to know? I'm sure you have questions."

*What exactly do you know about me?* "Um. Well, what are we doing here, for starters?"

Sloan smiled. "Having drinks." She raised her finger in the air to catch a waiter's attention. He hustled over and she looked at me. "What would you like?"

I thought quickly. "A glass of moscato, please."

She turned toward the waiter. "I'll have a dirty Grey Goose martini with 2 olives."

The waiter nodded and hurried away. Sloan put her chin in her hand and gazed at me expectantly. I fidgeted with my silverware.

"Boy, you really are a walking contradiction, aren't you?" Sloan said. "Ok, fine, I'll start. We're here to check out a new case. Have a first look at the subject."

I wasn't sure if I should be offended. "What do you mean, a walking contradiction?"

She looked me in the eye. "You're very passive for someone so inquisitive. You seem to want answers, but

the basics on who I was dealing with."

"So what was your conclusion?"

She sat in thought as she stared at her drink for a moment. "That you are very bright and driven, and have rarely ventured far from your tightly planned educational track. I think you ended up here with me because you've basically fulfilled your academic dreams, and yet still find something lacking. You need more."

I felt my cheeks redden with recognition. Maybe she *was* a witch after all. "I think it's possible you're onto something," I conceded.

"Well, that's where I come in. Just hang with me for a few days. See if anything interests you. I have a feeling you have it in you." She smiled. "And maybe I'm a little bored, too. So you'll be shaking things up for me as well."

I smiled back at her. "Fair enough."

Sloan picked up her glass and relaxed into her seat. I did the same. We sat quietly for a moment. I watched the crowd, lost in thought about the strange scenario I found myself in. It was already seeming less strange.

Sloan's voice interrupted my reverie. "Looks like we're on the move." She signaled the waiter.

I glanced over to see the man signing a credit card slip while his wife reapplied lipstick. The waiter delivered a similar slip to our table. Sloan quickly signed the bottom and handed it back. I looked at her inquisitively.

"I already set up the payment. Efficiency is key." She threw her bag over her shoulder and stood. "Ready?"

The couple was on their way out the door. I quickly grabbed my bag and followed.

\*\*\*

A few blocks from the restaurant, we stopped in the shadows and watched from a distance. The subjects of our surveillance had arrived on foot at their next destination, a local theater house. They stopped among the well-dressed patrons milling about outside.

"So this is definitely not the more typical get-your-hands-dirty case," Sloan whispered. "The client just wants him followed, so we follow. It could be a great way to introduce you to this sort of thing."

We watched the couple move toward the entrance, hand over their tickets and enter.

"Guess they were meeting for a drink until time for their play," Sloan said. "Just a wholesome date night."

"I assume we're not following them in?"

Sloan shook her head and reached up to unclasp her strand of pearls. "I don't think there's much chance he's going to get into any trouble while he's out with his wife. So that gives us plenty of time to take care of something else. Hopefully something a lot more fun."

She unbuttoned and shook off her cardigan to reveal an ultra-fitted black sheath dress. She looked stunning. Sloan stuffed the items in her bag and gave me a mischievous look. "Want to help me with a favor?"

# FIVE

In a trendy nearby restaurant teeming with nightlife, we grabbed a high top table in the back bar area. Sloan threw her bag on the stool. "Another glass of wine?"

"Sure."

Sloan made her way to the bar and caught the attention of the bartender immediately. I watched as she laughed amiably at some remark when he swiftly presented the drinks.

I raised my voice over the din of the bar when she returned with the drinks. "So what are we doing now?"

"We're here to see that guy." She nodded her head toward the bar.

"Who, the bartender?"

"Yep. I already knew just from his picture that the guy is probably a dirt bag. But I need to find out for sure for his girlfriend."

"Oh. So is she another client?"

Sloan shook her head. "It's for a source. Our client's

assistant. Her name's Hannah." She took a sip of her drink. "It was clear that Mr. Westbrook-the-elder wasn't going to be helpful enough for my taste. He wouldn't even let me see details of this deal that is supposed to be so important. Said it was top secret and irrelevant. So I made friends with his right-hand man. Secretly, of course."

I took a drink, still confused.

Sloan chuckled. "Actually, that's what you had inadvertently seen when you came to the conclusion I must be a Russian spy." She smiled in amusement. "Hannah agreed to pass along whatever deal information she had access to—which apparently was not much. I was retrieving the documents."

I thought back to the sight of Sloan pulling a manila envelope from the lining of the trashcan. "So why were they hidden?"

She grinned. "I made that up. She was worried about getting in trouble for helping, and I could tell that she would be into the whole cloak-and-dagger thing. It made her feel more secure by doing it in secret, but also made it exciting for her at the same time."

I could relate to that. "I guess everyone has a little bit of a spy fantasy."

"Seems like it. So when she confided that she was having doubts about a dutiful boyfriend she suspected was secretly a player, I offered to look into his moral character in exchange for a little help in getting the inside scoop in that company."

I looked over at the bar. The bartender was attractive in a generic frat-boy sort of way. He appeared in his mid-twenties, his tan face and brown eyes framed by expertly tousled blonde-highlighted hair. His grooming and fitted polo shirt with turned-up collar gave him a confident and moneyed air.

"His name is Blaine," Sloan said.

"Yeah, sounds about right."

Sloan laughed. "I really don't know anything else. I just figured we'd watch him for a bit, and then maybe get a feel for him up close."

I nodded, watching Blaine chat with customers. "I'm with you. I don't have much trouble picturing this guy being shady. I wonder what she sees in him."

"Not really your type, huh?" Sloan smiled. "So what is your type? You have a secret boyfriend I couldn't dig up?"

I shook my head. "Not seeing anyone at the moment. But if I were, he would definitely not be like this guy. Probably a little more—intellectual, I guess. And darker hair. Especially with light eyes."

Sloan smirked. "So, basically yourself."

I grimaced. "Disturbing. But yes, I suppose. Only a lot more masculine."

Sloan nodded her understanding.

"What about you? You with someone?"

"No. I was in a serious relationship for several years. He was pretty great." She shrugged. "Ever since that ended, I've found myself only attracted to bad boys."

"What, like criminals?"

She laughed and shook her head. "Like tough guys. Not steroidal gym-rats, but real, confident manly men. Motorcycles are a plus. But not too many tattoos."

I crinkled my nose. "Yeah, that's definitely not my type either."

"That's good. I don't really see them as long-term potential. But I guess that's the point for me."

She picked up her drink and gazed pensively at the surrounding crowd. I sensed I shouldn't pursue the topic any further for the time being. I kept an eye on the bar as I sipped my wine. I was starting to get a bit of a buzz.

Sloan seemed to perk up suddenly. "You need another drink?"

I shook my head. "Just started this one. I'm a little lightheaded as it is. Do you drink like this for all your jobs?"

"Nah," she replied. "A few sips makes the night go by, but I mainly just use them as a prop in places like these. But having you along tonight makes it much more social. I like it."

Sloan hopped from her stool and smoothed her dress. "I think it's time to have a little chat with Mr. Bartender. We're going to need to flirt with him just a little. I want to see how he handles."

I was suddenly a little uneasy. Sitting back and watching was one thing; I wasn't sure I was ready to participate in any deceptions.

She seemed to sense my hesitation. "Or we could try it another way—you could pretend to be my girlfriend. I'll do all the talking." Her smile was devious. "That might work even better for a guy like that. Plus it always makes for an easy exit. "

I laughed as I felt my face redden. "I don't think so. How about if I stay here and just watch this time?"

Her face seemed to fall ever so slightly, but she smiled to cover it. "Sure, no problem."

Suddenly I had an idea. "What if I just listened for now?"

Sloan shook her head. "Sorry, I don't have any kind of surveillance devices with me."

I dug my phone out of my purse and fired up the application I needed. I handed her the phone.

"Just take my phone with you. I'll be able to hear everything."

She frowned. "I'm afraid it might seem suspicious if you're pretending to be on the phone the whole time. And I don't think you'd hear that well."

I grinned, pleased with myself. "I don't need a phone. I'll hear every word and I guarantee no one will be able to tell."

Sloan looked thoroughly confused. "You brought a listening device?"

"Yes, the ones I use every day. Only I call them hearing aids."

I pulled back the hair behind my ear to show her one of the devices.

"They help me hear some high-pitch sounds I'm missing," I explained. "But now they can do some tricks, like letting me stream sound into my ears from across the room."

Her jaw dropped. She examined my ear. "I had no idea you were wearing anything."

She took several steps away and whispered discreetly into the phone. "So you can hear me from over here?" Her voice dropped to a dramatic whisper. "The eagle flies at midnight."

I laughed. "Yes, Bond."

She returned to the table, grinning with amusement.

"But you won't need to talk into the phone," I said. "It can pick up from all around. Just put it on the bar in front of you."

Her eyes twinkled. "Oh, this is fantastic. Very convenient. I can think of many ways this will come in handy."

"Let's just try it out for now. Go do your thing, and I'll listen and learn."

"You got it." She sauntered off and hopped onto a stool at the bar. The crowd had thinned, allowing Blaine to attend to her immediately.

"Boy am I glad you're thirsty tonight," he said. "What else can I get you?"

"Actually, I just need a water for my friend. I think she's had a little too much to drink."

It felt very strange, listening to the conversation that Blaine thought was private. I felt a little stab of guilt. But it was also invigorating to know that no one else in the room had any idea what I was up to. Our little secret.

Sloan kept him busy with some banter. I could tell she was holding back, taking care not to be forward. She was just being friendly and giving him an opportunity to take it further, if so inclined.

He seemed to be so inclined. For his part, Blaine played it cool, fidgeting with bar items in the vicinity to look busy while he chatted. But his eyes belied his nonchalance. When Sloan slid off her barstool after a few minutes, he looked momentarily crushed.

"So wait . . . listen, you have a boyfriend?"

"No," Sloan replied, flippant again. She grabbed the bottle of water. "But I better get my friend home. What do I owe you?"

"Don't worry about it. You can pay me back next time." His grin was almost charming.

Sloan gave the charm right back. "Ok. Well, thanks."

He watched her return to the table. I marveled at her magnetism.

"That was incredible," I said. "Practically all you did was smile at him."

"It's mainly confidence. With some practice and a little styling, I think we could get you going in no time."

I blushed at the thought. Sloan handed me the bottle of water.

"Here, drink some of this. Then I think I'm ready to call it a night. You?"

"Sure." I complied and we gathered our things.

Sloan paused for a moment. "No drinking next time, I promise. You in?"

Amazingly, I didn't have to think. I just smiled in answer and headed for the exit.

# SIX

Luckily two glasses of wine may have given me a buzz, but they didn't lead to a hangover. I woke Sunday morning refreshed, looking forward to the day. I couldn't believe I had fallen into something so unlike me, and so quickly. One day I was bored, reading about surveillance in my novels, and the next I was secretly listening in on conversations. And I felt alive.

But I found myself wishing for that hangover on Monday morning. I could've used the excuse to stay home and avoid the new reality that awaited me at work. The reality that assailed me as soon as I walked in the door.

"You *must* be Quinn," an exuberant male voice sounded from the corner of the small intern office.

I turned to find a young man approaching me. Trim, lithe, and well-dressed. A little too well-dressed.

"Hi," I offered tentatively, unsure who was invading my space.

"I'm Grant," he gushed. "And I'm your new co-intern. Sooo glad to meet you."

Okay, now I was certain. Definitely gay. *I love gay men.*

And then he opened his mouth again. "Well, aren't you too cute with your plain-Jane shoes and old-lady sweater. You don't need to be fashionable *and* smart. I'll bet you take your brains very seriously. I better watch out."

Old-lady sweater! It was just a cardigan. A form-fitted, expensive cardigan I found very flattering.

I was still processing when my boss entered the room. "Oh good, I see you two have met."

"Just getting there." I forced a smile and reached my hand to the galling newcomer. "Nice to meet you."

"Grant is your new fellow fourth-year intern," she continued. "You two will share this office. Grant, you can have that desk." She pointed to the unused workstation right next to mine.

Grant's voice was far too enthusiastic for first thing in the morning. "Office mates! It'll be great."

*Sounds great already.*

Dr. Seymore placed a hand on his shoulder. "Grant comes to us from an excellent school in the Midwest, and has a very inspiring story. From troubled adolescent to doctoral candidate in a just a few short years. It's very impressive. I hope you two will learn a lot from each other."

"I'm sure we will."

"Okay, I'll leave you to get settled in. Grant, your orientation starts in 15 minutes." She turned and headed back to her office.

"I'll be there with bells on," he called after her.

I sucked up my initial reservations about the situation and offered some opening friendliness. "So, you're new to Virginia?"

"Yes, it's crazy. It's sooo different here. Very quaint. Nobody cares what the rest of the world is doing. You look like you fit right in, though."

"Um. Yeah, I guess."

"Good for you. I'm so glad they take students like you too, not just from the very top-tier schools. Everyone deserves a chance to learn, I say."

Utterly without words, all I could do was force my lips into a brief smile. Thankfully Grant turned his attention to his new desk, giving a little squeal as he settled into his chair.

*How was that even possible?* I'm pretty sure every friendly comment was actually a dig—and an unfounded one, at that. This wasn't exactly the backwoods. And I went to a great school.

Yes, I loved gay men, but they never seemed to love me back. I'm not quite fabulous enough. I bet they just *love* Sloan. I escaped in search of some coffee. I would need to stock up. Too bad a minibar was frowned upon at the office.

\*\*\*

I would be flying solo for our next gig, at least at first. I had agreed to begin some routine surveillance for Sloan after work, while she was busy closing out another case. Our target was frequently known to work late, and I was simply to find out where he goes when he leaves. Sloan would catch up and take over in a bit.

The rest of my workday had flown by in anticipation of a little excitement, despite Sloan's warnings that not every watch leads somewhere interesting. The prospect had also kept me from musing too long about my new officemate. Luckily, he had been absorbed in his orientation duties the rest of the day, so I got a little break from the charming fellow.

I pulled into the Westbrook parking lot and wedged my car between two others at the back of the lot. Walter Westbrook's vehicle was indeed sitting in his marked space at the front. Next to it was a car with an oddly-shaped item on the hood. I studied it from afar and decided that the shoots sticking out were flower stems. I picked up the phone to check in with Sloan.

"He's here. By the way, I know you said the client drives a Porsche. Does Richard also have a silver Mercedes?"

"Don't think so. Why?"

"One is parked in his reserved space. And it has

something sitting against the windshield. Looks like some kind of flower arrangement."

"I don't think that's him. As far as I know, he's gone for the day. Let me call Richard's assistant back and find out. Can you go check out whatever it is?"

"Okay." I disconnected and checked my surroundings. After normal office hours, the campus was quiet. I slipped out of my car and made my way toward the front of the lot, playing with my phone to look occupied. That allowed me to casually snap a photo of the license plate and then the large bouquet I found splayed across the windshield.

But I had to drop the pretense briefly to inspect the item. There was a small card tucked into the arrangement of tropical flowers. Unfortunately, it was sealed.

A quick glance in the car windows also turned up nothing. The car was obsessively clean inside. I returned to my car, once again ensuring that no one else was in sight. A few minutes later my phone rang.

"It's the CEO of the other company," Sloan said. "She showed up unexpectedly, supposedly to talk to Walter about their deal. Hannah will keep watch for us, and let us know if anything looks less than businesslike."

"Great."

"Just stay put. You might be able to catch the parting if they come out together. If they think they're alone, we should be able to tell their relationship. I'll be there as soon as I can."

We ended the call and I returned my attention to the front of the building. It would be dark soon, giving me better cover for my surveillance. The waiting was an odd combination of boring and exciting at the same time. Just the idea that something might turn up somehow made it worth it.

It was nearly an hour later when I perked up. A few stranglers had wandered out in the interim. But I now recognized Walter exiting the building, accompanied by a woman with dark, layered shoulder-length hair. I pulled out the camera Sloan had loaned me. It was smaller than those I had seen PIs use in movies, but still seemed to be pretty powerful. The pictures would certainly be better than those from my cell phone. I used it to zoom in on our targets and watch.

The woman seemed a similar age as her companion, but much more put-together. Her fitted dark suit and heels gave her a commanding presence. And as I focused in on her face, I realized I knew that commanding presence. I grabbed my phone and dialed Sloan again.

I got right to it when she answered. "What is the name of the company doing the deal with Westbrook?"

"Quandom Corp—they're a tech and fiber-optic company," she replied. "Why?"

*Oh no.* "I never knew that was who we were talking about. This is Carolyn Evans."

"That's right," Sloan said. "How did you know?"

I kept an eye on our targets. Their pace had slowed as

they neared the cars and spotted the bouquet. My stomach sank as I watched.

"She's on my dissertation committee," I said. "My research project will take place at their facility."

"No way. So you know her?"

"We've met. At my proposal meeting. But she was just a high-level manager at the time."

"That's right, it's temporary. She became acting CEO a couple months ago. That's about all I know so far."

The woman seemed to hesitate uncertainly as she approached the car. She definitely didn't look like someone excited to receive a surprise from a loved one. Walter stayed back and watched, seeming only mildly interested. The woman pulled the card from the display and opened it. I snapped some photos of the scene.

"Well, it doesn't look like our guy has anything to do with the flowers," I said. "And she doesn't seem very happy to see them."

After checking the card, the woman grabbed up the armful of flowers and threw them hastily in her backseat. She then gave a quick wave to Walter and climbed behind the wheel. I returned my attention to Sloan. "She's leaving."

"Follow her."

"But I thought we're watching Walter."

"We were," she said. "But if she happens to go see whoever sent her the flowers, we can show evidence to the client that she's not seeing Walter. Cross one possibility off our list."

I bit my lip, thinking. "If I get caught, this woman could ruin my study. And thus, my career."

"You won't get caught. Just follow her in the car. I'll head your way now and try to catch up. You won't even have to get out."

I watched the woman turn out of the parking lot and knew I only had an instant to decide. Despite my reservations, I started the car and began my first solo tail.

My tail of the woman holding my future in her hands.

# SEVEN

"She's taking the exit." My voice sounded unintentionally anxious. "Where are you?"

Sloan was much calmer. "Almost there. Stay on her."

I kept my distance when the Mercedes exited the interstate, but knew I would have to get closer as we neared the busy shopping area. The woman turned directly into the heart of the town center. A hotel tower loomed overhead. I informed Sloan of our position, and then hesitated when the woman turned into the parking garage next door. Sloan urged me to continue.

I followed the woman to the third level of the public garage. When she began to pull into a parking space, I froze for a moment. *How do I continue from here without being seen?* I didn't have any specialized training in this sort of thing.

"She's going to see me in the parking garage. How do I do this?"

No response.

"Sloan?" I checked my phone when she didn't answer. I had lost signal in the parking structure. I was on my own.

I drove past my target and continued around the corner, where a spot was open out of sight of the lower level. I quickly parked and slipped out of the car as noiselessly as possible. Peeking around the bend, I saw the woman was heading for the elevator.

I obviously couldn't ride with her in the elevator. I glanced around the garage for an alternative. There was a stairwell entrance nearby. I would have to take my chances that she was going in the most likely direction. Down.

I watched until the elevator doors opened and then ran for the stairs. When I opened the door at the bottom, I found myself walking into a trendy hotel lobby. I was exposed and needed to find a way to hide. I threw myself onto one of the many clustered sofas and picked up a magazine. I would have to get some advice on disguises in the future.

A ding sounded from my left. I kept my head down, letting my hair hide my face as the woman exited the garage elevator and crossed the lobby behind me. She stopped in front of another bank of elevators that ascended into the hotel tower.

I felt a stab of disappointment that I had come this far, and wouldn't be able to figure out where she was going. But there was no way I could race the elevator up on foot, especially without knowing the floor.

A quiet but familiar voice sounded behind me. "Which way?"

I turned to see Sloan, her hair hidden under a black fedora. I'm sure the surprise showed on my face. "How did you catch up so fast?"

"Left my car with valet," she said. "Which way?"

I nodded my head toward the woman across the lobby. Sloan headed her way without another word.

When they both disappeared into the elevator, I mulled what my next move should be. I didn't want to stay here, exposed for no reason. I could take the opportunity to check the woman's car again with no chance of being seen. I retraced my steps back to the garage.

I got lucky when I returned to the Mercedes. The flowers were splayed in the back floorboard. On the seat above them lay the accompanying card, the message visible. I couldn't quite make out the writing, so I fetched the camera from my car and snapped a photo before returning to the safety of my vehicle.

I pulled up the photo while I waited. After zooming in, I could clearly read the note. Whoever sent the flowers missed Carolyn Evans terribly, was dying to see her, and hoped she would forgive them. It ended with a room number at the hotel. The note wasn't signed. I wondered what Sloan was able to discover on the twenty-second floor.

A few minutes later she appeared, walking up the garage ramp. She spotted my car and hopped in. "Glad she didn't decide to park at the top," Sloan said. "It would take forever to find you."

"So what did you find out?"

She grinned. "I'm starved. Let's go grab something to eat. I know just the place."

"Fine." I couldn't help my grin back at her. Despite my reservations, I was having a blast.

*** 

I laughed at myself as I followed her into the parking lot of Joe's Diner, recalling my first assumptions about Sloan. *Russian spy.* But so far the truth was just as exciting, only legal. I hoped.

The waitress from my first visit approached with a wide smile as we settled into the booth at the back. "Welcome back."

"Oh." I was surprised she remembered me. "Thanks."

"This is Dottie," Sloan said. "She was expecting you the first time you came in. Dottie had strict instructions not to give out any information on that receipt."

Dottie chuckled lightly. "Yeah, sorry about that. But I see it all got straightened out."

Sloan turned to the waitress. "This is my new friend Quinn. She's going to be helping me."

"Real nice to meet you, Quinn. Any friend of Ms. McKenzie is a friend of ours." She handed me a menu.

"Good to meet you too."

Dottie wandered away to let me look over the menu. Not surprisingly, Sloan didn't seem to need one. I decided on a pot pie and returned my attention to my companion.

"So I take it you come here a lot."

"You could say that. My office is just down the road, where you dropped me off. I've been coming here for years. We help each other out."

Before I could ask what she meant, Dottie returned with a carafe of coffee and poured each of us a cup.

She sighed. "I know I might as well leave this here with you." She sat the carafe next to Sloan on the table.

We gave our orders and Dottie again disappeared.

I looked at Sloan expectantly. "So what did you find?"

She pulled out her phone to show me a photo. A man with an unkempt beard and overlong salt-and-pepper hair stood in the hotel room doorway in front of Carolyn Evans. "She's visiting with this shaggy man in there. But just like the flowers, she didn't look pleased to see him at first."

She scrolled to pictures of the woman entering the room. The man was wrapping his arms around her. "But as you can see, she did give in. He was apparently pretty persuasive."

"Well, it looks like she had reason to not be happy to see him." I pulled out the camera and showed Sloan the photograph of the note. "He wants forgiveness for something. Any idea who he is?"

"No, I haven't done any research on her yet. But it may

not matter. I assume Walter saw the flowers. Did he react to them?"

I shook my head. "Not at all."

"Well, that seems unlikely if they had any sort of romantic relationship. So now I can give Richard evidence they aren't involved. If someone is manipulating Walter to get a deal, it doesn't look like it's her."

"Great." I glanced at the photos again. They were from fairly close range. "But how did you hang around the room unnoticed?"

"I wasn't unnoticed, just dismissed. Got lucky. When I got off the elevator first, I saw a couple leaving their room. So once they were out of sight, I banged on their door, hoping no one else was in there. After a few tries, I slid to the floor in obvious frustration, waiting for them." She grinned. "The targets never paid me a bit of attention."

"I'll remember that."

"I don't think it's very important who she's seeing in there, just that it's not Walter. But just in case, I planted a tiny motion-sensor camera in front of the room. I'll get an emailed photo every time someone passes by. And whenever she leaves."

*Planting hidden cameras?* I was amazed that this was considered an occupation. I didn't even want to think about the legality of that right now.

Dottie appeared with our food. Starved, I dug in.

"Nice work today," Sloan said, cutting up her pancakes. "I'll set up a meeting with Richard to go over this tomorrow. As one of the contributing photographers, you should be there." She narrowed her eyes playfully. "But we don't have to tell him that."

# EIGHT

I recognized him immediately from the photo. He had the slicked-back dark hair I expected, although the graying temples were now suspiciously missing. His fine dark suit was straining at the seams, and his face was a little shiny with perspiration.

The man looked out of place as he huffed his way through the worn diner. He took a seat facing the front, just as we anticipated. This allowed me a perfect view of Richard Westbrook from across the diner.

Dottie hurried over, pausing to watch him inspect the table with a grimace.

She approached with feigned timidity. "Would you like me to clean it again, sir?"

"No point." Richard glared at the booth. "You can't fix old and run down with a rag." He looked up at her impatiently. "I need coffee."

Her smiled was perky, in spite of his brusqueness. "Coming right up."

Dottie winked at me as she passed. I returned my eyes to my book and waited. She was just pouring Richard his cup of coffee when I had a sudden influx of sound in my ears. Sloan had turned on my streaming as she entered.

She strolled quickly to his table and slid opposite him in the booth, facing away from me. With the small remote microphone I had given her clipped to her purse, we would no longer even need her to carry my phone. I would hear everything clearly from my table, streamed into my hearing aids. Gotta love technology.

"Would you like some coffee too, miss?" Dottie said.

"Sure."

Dottie poured a second cup and looked up expectantly. "Now, can I get either of you somethin' to eat?"

"I hear they have excellent apple pie," Sloan offered.

"Pass." Richard waved his hand dismissively at Dottie, eyes fixed on Sloan. "You're late."

Sloan shot a quick smile up. "Just the coffee then, thanks."

She proceeded to ignore Richard while she busied herself with cream and sugar. I admired her composure.

Finally Richard's impatience broke in. "Well? You said you had some information for me?"

"I do. Unfortunately, nothing directly on your brother yet." She took a sip of her coffee.

"So why am I here?"

Sloan gazed back coolly. "I thought you might be interested to know it's not very likely Walter is involved with the CEO you mentioned. I saw nothing between them when they were alone together. I'm pretty certain there's nothing there."

Richard simply blinked at her.

Sloan continued. "And then there was evidence she's involved with someone else."

She paused as she noticed the same change in demeanor I did. Richard had stiffened and was glaring at her intently. She continued carefully. "So I don't think you need to worry about Walter and Carolyn Evans."

"Someone else . . . who?"

"I don't know yet. I didn't think the *who* was important."

"It's not," Richard retorted. "But what evidence?"

Sloan pulled photos from her bag and handed them across the table. I could tell from a glance that the first was my photo of the bouquet on the CEO's car. Richard examined it closely.

Sloan narrated. "After she found that waiting for her in the parking lot last night, she drove straight to a hotel."

Richard flipped to the next picture. I knew it captured Carolyn outside the mystery man's hotel room. The final photo would show the man grasping her suggestively as they disappeared into the room.

"She was there for a couple of hours," Sloan continued.

I watched in fascination as the color drained from Richard's face. He studied the photos for a long moment, then slammed them on the table, his color returning. "Why were you following this woman? This is not your assignment."

"Oh." Sloan sounded genuinely surprised. "I thought you were concerned about her and Walter having a possible relationship." She pointed to the picture. "This way we can pretty much rule out that complication. Your brother didn't even react to the flowers."

"You don't need to worry about motivations." Richard was overtly hostile now. "Your job is to keep an eye on Walter, and capture anything suspicious. Keep your nose out of anything else. I'm not paying you to run around following whoever you want."

Sloan took the rebuke calmly. "Got it."

"In fact, you need to bring me anything even remotely suggestive. I need to know it all. It's not your job to judge whether there's anything there or not. Leave that to me."

Sloan plucked her phone from her purse and spoke with feigned deference. "I'm going to take notes, so I can make sure to get you exactly what you want." She began typing. "So you want . . . everything? Like, if he's a little too friendly with a woman? Or even if she's just flirting with him?"

"Anything," Richard snapped. "I'll be the judge."

My phone vibrated next to me. I tapped it under the table to reveal a text from Sloan.

*SOMETHING'S UP. LEAVE NOW AND FOLLOW *

Sloan continued with her guileless questions to keep

Richard talking. I left some money on the table and slipped out. My connection to their conversation dropped out as I exited.

I waited in my car, once again parked in the grocery lot next door. I didn't have to wait long before Richard stomped out and squeezed himself into his sports car. I had no time to consider my nervousness in undertaking the tail of this hostile man. Once he had pulled out of the parking lot, I was hot in pursuit.

***

I had followed Sloan's advice about keeping my distance, but it wasn't easy. Richard treated other drivers with the same respect he offered in person. He weaved in and out of traffic impatiently, nearly causing collisions as he frequently swerved in front of other cars. But I was still able to keep him in view without all the dramatic maneuvers.

The sun had finished setting during the drive, giving me some additional cover. We arrived in a wealthy established neighborhood, where the landscaped lawns were expansive and well-tended and the houses were even more generous. I picked up my phone and dialed Sloan to check in.

She picked up immediately, excitement in her voice. "Still with him?"

"Yes, but I don't know if he's just going home or not. He's

pulling into a driveway ahead." I checked the street name and notified Sloan before continuing slowly past the house.

"No, that's not his address. Hang on." I could hear her typing rapidly in the background.

Richard was storming up the sidewalk of the stately two-story colonial, folded papers in his hand. My stomach twisted in excitement as I realized they were probably the photographs Sloan had provided.

Sloan's voice was also clearly excited when she returned. "It's Carolyn's house!"

"I had a feeling. And I think he's taken the pictures with him. Maybe he's actually the one having an affair with her." I stopped the car down the street to think, the front of the house now out of view.

"And we just informed him that someone else is in the picture. Literally." Sloan paused, considering. "He could be confronting her. But this doesn't seem like it has anything to do with his brother, does it?"

*What had we stumbled upon?* "Not at the moment. So what do we do now?"

"You're going to have to go check it out."

*Uh oh.* "What do you mean?"

"You need to sneak up to the house. Check if you can see them through a window."

I glanced around the empty street, my heart beginning to race. As fun as that sounded, this woman knew me. I couldn't risk getting caught snooping.

"You'll need to hurry," Sloan continued. "Make sure

she's not getting murdered or something. I wouldn't put it past him."

*Murder!* I couldn't live with causing something bad to happen and not doing anything about it. *Could I?*

"Put on the hat and sweatshirt I told you to carry," Sloan continued to prod.

I retrieved the dark baseball cap and hoodie. They did make me feel more discreet once I had them on. My resistance wavered. After another moment of hesitation, I decided to just go for it.

"Ok, hang on." I slipped out of the car and crept across the lawn, which was damp from the sprinkler system. Thankfully it was not currently running. The front rooms were all dark, so I headed for a lighted window in the back.

Peeking in the window, I saw a den with overstuffed leather furniture and dark wood. The sheer curtains did little to hamper my view. I first thought the room was unoccupied and was going to keep searching. Then I noticed Richard standing unmoving in the corner. Arms crossed, he was fuming silently.

A moment later Carolyn entered the room carrying drinks. Richard swatted away the offered glass, so she placed it patiently on a table beside him.

He retrieved the stack of photographs and waved them in the air in indignation. I snapped a photo of the scene with my phone. Unfortunately, my clear view didn't include sound. I couldn't make out what he was saying, or more likely yelling.

But if I couldn't hear them, they wouldn't be able to hear me. I moved away from the window and spoke quietly.

"Okay, I can see them. He's with Carolyn, and he's clearly angry about the pictures. She seems to be trying to calm him down and explain something. But I can't hear."

"Do they seem like lovers? Yuck, by the way."

I peeked back through the window. Richard had drained his drink and was intently listening to Carolyn. She looked grim as she spoke.

"Not really," I replied. "Him being jealous is the only thing that makes sense right now, but so far I don't see any sign of romance. They sure don't look very intimate."

Richard began to pace the room, anger etched on his face. His perspiration had increased with the exertion. I watched in silence for a while as they continued back and forth, Richard barking at the woman while she tried to respond calmly. But she seemed just as serious and possibly worried. She began to pace.

Frustrated by the lack of insight being gleaned from this operation, I decided to try moving closer to see if I could pick up on their conversation. They were standing near a window on the other side of the room. I moved carefully around the corner of the house.

A large flower bed extended along the side of the residence. I attempted to navigate the assorted plants, wishing I could use my phone as a flashlight, but I was afraid of drawing attention. Apparently I didn't need a light for that. My foot caught on an offshoot of some sort, sending me tumbling to the ground.

"Oof."

I scrambled to extricate myself from the plants and quickly brushed away the mulch lodged in my hands, thinking my quiet accident would be able to go undetected.

"Someone there?"

Instantly, a light was searching the flower bed. The beam quickly found me and I squinted from the glare. It was coming from the yard next door. *Crap!* Think fast.

"Hi," I answered and waved with forced friendliness. With the light on me, I was able to move through the flower bed and away from the window easily. I approached the older woman slowly with my hands clearly visible. She stood in her driveway, holding her large dog's leash protectively.

I heard Sloan's voice in my ear, still connected. "Quinn? What's going on?"

I ignored her and jumped in before the woman could speak again. "Have you seen Mr. Snuffaluffagus?"

The woman eyed me suspiciously. "Mister Whatagus?"

"Mr. Snuffaluffagus. My cat." I glanced around as if searching. "He got out, and I thought I saw him running through here."

"I didn't see any cat." The woman nodded her head toward her dog. "And Oscar here would've noticed."

"Oh, shoot! I bet that's what scared him off again. Mr. Snuffaluffagus is terrified of dogs."

She just blinked at me, unsure how to respond.

"I'm just so worried," I rambled quickly. "He's never really gotten out before. And it's time for his medicine. I better keep looking. Would you keep an eye out for him?"

The woman hesitated, but only momentarily. "Sure."

"Thanks." I rushed across the front yard before she could respond further. I called out when I reached the street. "Mr. Snuffaluffagus!"

Once in my car, I remembered I still had Sloan on the line. She had stayed silent through the confrontation.

"I gotta go, Sloan."

"That was some quick thinking. Good instincts."

"Talk to you later." I hung up, utterly drained.

When I turned the car on, I realized the hidden benefit of driving a hybrid vehicle. I was able to start the car and begin my escape silently, with no engine to alert the neighborhood. I turned my lights on a block away.

My hands stopped shaking at some point on the way home.

# NINE

The next two days passed very slowly as I fought a battle inside my head. Back at work, I tried to absorb myself in my patient schedule of hearing and balance problems. But whenever I had a break in the day, my mind would inevitably wander back to the investigation. Sloan's regular text updates certainly didn't help my concentration.

The morning after my close encounter at the CEO's house, I had woken determined to stay away from the mischief. The investigation, all fun and games in the beginning, had turned into a threat against my career. If I had been caught by the neighbor, it could've been disastrous.

I had no idea how I would've explained spying in her windows to Carolyn Evans. But regardless of my explanation, she likely would have pulled support for my research project. And that could mean not being able to graduate, certainly not on time anyway.

So I sent a message to Sloan I was going to be busy and wouldn't be able to help for a while. Eventually I would sever my involvement completely. It was a fun fantasy while it lasted, but sneaking around at night to peek in windows didn't really fit the profile of a respected medical professional. And that's what I needed to focus on.

But Sloan was not to be dissuaded so easily. Every couple of hours my phone vibrated, and I knew she was sending me more information. Trying to get me to stay engrossed. She had been doing more stalking, and had turned up some information on the mysterious interloper in the hotel room.

It turned out that the subject of Richard's wrath was actually the woman's ex-husband. According to Sloan, he was not easily identified at first because he was fresh out of rehab. Apparently the addiction had done a number on his appearance, because the gaunt, shaggy-haired man in the hotel photos looked nothing like the handsome, athletic middle-aged man in the before-pictures Sloan had sent me.

So it seemed Richard had been furious that Carolyn went to visit her recently-rehabilitated ex. The flowers and handsiness suggested reconciliation. I still found it hard to believe Richard had been passionate out of jealousy, or that she would have been involved with him. But I suppose all manner of blowhards find romance somehow. Especially wealthy ones.

But that was really none of my concern; I was here to help my patients hear better. And get my diploma. That was all that should matter.

At lunchtime on day three, Sloan really started blowing up my phone. No more details, just pleas to meet. They became more urgent as the day went on. I was going to have to be more forceful in my disinterest.

When my phone buzzed once more in the afternoon, I checked it at my desk between patients.

*YOU HAVE TO MEET ME TONIGHT. LIFE OR DEATH*

Life or death? Seemed a tad overdramatic.

There was no reason to drag this out. I needed to extricate myself from this situation before it distracted me any further. I typed a reply.

*JOE'S, 6PM.*

I received a prompt emoticon in agreement just as I heard Grant enter our work area from behind.

"Wowzers." He broke the silence with his whine. "I don't have the nerve to break the rules and do personal stuff on the clock. I'm too afraid it'll reflect poorly if the boss sees me. Good for you for being so *brave*."

Well, it wouldn't be my office anymore without a grating voice hassling me in the background. I gritted my teeth before looking up with a fake smile. "Just something quick I had to take care of. All caught up now."

Grant ignored my response and launched into a gossipy story about his annoying roommate. *Boy, talk about lacking self-awareness.*

Certain he would never notice if I was actually listening or not, I surreptitiously clicked the music app on my phone, and classical music began playing softly in my ears. I felt better instantly. Apparently my little helper devices were good for more than just eavesdropping conversations. They also kept me from strangling my coworker.

Now I just had to keep my nerve until this evening. I knew what I had to do, but now that I had put a plan in motion, I felt a small knot forming in my stomach. It could've been a feeling of disappointment, if I were being honest with myself.

But that kind of honesty was the last thing I needed.

*** 

Sloan was waiting with two cups of coffee when I arrived. I immediately sensed that she was missing her usual perkiness that evening. Her eyes were more guarded and serious than I'd seen before. *Maybe because I've been dodging her for a few days.* I felt a little stab of guilt as I slid into the booth across from her.

"Listen," I began.

"I know," Sloan interrupted. "I know you think you need to quit the spying business. But first, let me just show you a few things." Her eyes were imploring. "Please."

I had to give in. "Okay." I noted that my coffee was

already lightened to a pale beige with cream, just the way I liked it. I sat back and took a sip, waiting for her to begin.

"Okay. To recap, we now know the man at the hotel was Carolyn's ex-husband. And we witnessed Richard flipping out after seeing pictures of her with the guy, rushing straight to her house. Thanks to you, we know they had a long, heated conversation. But we don't know what about or why."

"Right."

"Well, the strung-out looking ex-husband is Carter Evans. He wasn't always a loser and he's not officially an Ex yet. He was actually the CEO of Quandom. It was his company she works for. Until his drug habit became impossible to hide any longer, that is. Pain killer addiction after a surgery." She took a sip of her coffee. "Anyway, the company allowed Carolyn to step in in his place, while he was shipped off to extended rehab on the company's dime. In the meantime he was served with separation papers. Can't say I blame her."

"Okay." I was unsure where this was going.

"Just bear with me." Sloan she pulled photos from her bag. "So apparently this recently-separated husband checked himself out of rehab a little ahead of schedule. I'm guessing that's why Richard was so surprised to see him in the pictures."

"And the hotel makes sense," I mused out loud, "because he can't go home anymore and probably doesn't have a housing plan just yet." I was annoyed with myself for being interested.

She nodded. "But I'm thinking that without a home and your life in shambles, it's pretty easy to get yourself back into trouble." Sloan placed two of the photographs side by side on the table. The first showed Carter sitting at a bar with a beer in front of him. In the second, he appeared to be taking a shot of liquor. "Doesn't look like he's sticking to that sobriety too well. I think they frown upon getting drunk within days of rehab. This was taken at the hotel bar last night."

I was letting myself be drawn in again; I had no reason to care about this drama. "Listen, I just can't get involved. This man's soon-to-be ex-wife has the power to ruin my career. She could set me back at least a year in graduating, and I bet she wouldn't hesitate to do so if she found out I was following her around. She's not someone I want to mess with. So I have to end this. No more."

"I understand completely. But here's the thing: he's not her soon-to-be ex-husband anymore. He's her *deceased* husband."

I put my coffee down slowly, unsure I had understood. "*Deceased?* What do you mean . . . I thought these pictures were from last night."

"They were. It seems that drinking wasn't all he did last night. He later overdosed in his hotel room. They found him this morning."

"That's horrible."

Sloan nodded somberly.

I looked at the man in the photos again. "Well, he was an addict. You saw him relapsing yourself. It's very sad, but I don't know what it has to do with us."

Sloan narrowed her eyes. "You don't find it just the slightest bit suspicious?"

I hesitated, unsure. "Why, do you have any reason to believe there's something suspicious about it? Did Richard or his wife go there that night?"

"No. But someone did." Sloan laid another stack of photos on the table.

I recognized the slightly ajar door on the first image and whispered. "The camera you planted outside the hotel room?"

Sloan nodded. "That's how I found out about his death. I started receiving constant photos of activity going on. It looks like the maid found him. Then the authorities arrived. It wasn't long before they took him away. No big to-do, no crime scene tape. Open and shut case to them."

"But you're not so sure."

She shrugged. "The night he died, I snapped photos of him drinking. The camera planted in the hall tells me he went back to his room a couple of hours later, looking inebriated."

Sloan turned to the next photo, showing the man in the doorway to his room. In front of him stood a thin male with his back to the camera. He was wearing an oversized navy hooded sweatshirt and ripped jeans.

She continued. "Soon after, this mystery guy shows up and comes in for a while. It's about 3 a.m. when he leaves again. Here's a better look at him." She flipped over the final photo, of the visitor on his way out. He looked young, maybe early twenties, with greasy hair and multiple facial piercings.

Sloan pointed to his sweatshirt, where there was a logo of Japanese characters printed in white along the arms. "I didn't pay attention to him at the time, but this sleeve is in the photos at the bar, drinking next to Carter. They could've met there."

I looked at Sloan with skepticism. "Or that could easily be a friend or his dealer. It's very sad, but I still don't know what it has to do with us."

"It's true, it could be." Sloan looked me carefully in the eye. "But you don't find it suspicious that the ex–husband shows back up—Richard is clearly angry about it for some reason—and two days later the man is dead?"

I thought about it. "It's a little suspicious, I guess. But again, he was an addict. We can't jump to any conclusions." I felt uneasy talking about someone's death so clinically. "And now I certainly don't need to be involved any further. I can't be anywhere near this man's death."

"But I don't want to jump to conclusions. I want to find out the truth. Because if anything funny did happen we may be involved, whether we like it or not."

*I don't like the sound of that.* "What do you mean?"

Sloan pulled the rest of the photos from her lap and laid them in a stack in front of me. "The night after you peeped in Carolyn's house, while you were busy dodging me—I followed Richard to see what else he was up to."

In the first photo I could make out Richard, but I couldn't place the other man. He was almost as big as Richard, but his bulk looked stronger, more powerful. A shadow of salt and pepper stubble covered his lower face. Their dark suits looked out of place in what appeared to be an alley of some sort.

"Who is that?"

Sloan shook her head. "Don't know yet." She pointed to the picture. "But this is Richard pulling out a large wad of cash. He hands it over the mystery man—late at night between two deserted buildings."

I eyed the photo more closely. "Sort of an odd place for two well-dressed men to conduct business."

She nodded and turned to the next photo, showing Richard reaching his hand to the other man. "They have a tense little discussion. In the end, Richard hands him something else, small like a business card or a note, and they go on their separate ways. I wasn't able to follow the man in time without being detected. I had to sneak a little ways on foot just to get the pictures."

I tried to sort out the situation. "I'm still not following. This does seem weird, but what does it have do with everything?"

"It's the timeline. We show the pictures to Richard, unwittingly alerting him that Carolyn's husband is back. He rushes to her in a fury to discuss it. The following night, he's handing over cash to a seedy character in a dark alley." She picked up her coffee and sat back in her seat. "Less than thirty-six hours later, this same husband is found dead."

My stomach sank. When you put it that way, it was impossible to ignore the possibility that something more had taken place.

Sloan shrugged. "Maybe it's all a coincidence. But I can't ignore the fact that if something did happen, we played a part in this. We gave Richard the photos that could've set off the entire chain of events."

The reality of that set in. I felt a wave of guilt for having ever gotten involved in the first place.

"We need to take this to the police then. Let them sort it out."

Sloan shook her head. "Can't. First of all, the hidden camera at the hotel was totally illegal. Those pictures are just for us. But I'd also never work again if I went straight to the police with incomplete information—information I obtained while tailing my own client. If it turned out to not be true, no one would ever trust me to investigate for them. I have to find out the truth first." She shrugged. "Besides, do you really want to notify Carolyn Evans that we were following her and her husband, before we're sure what happened?"

She had a point. "But what if he did it?"

"If we find evidence that Richard had anything to do with this, I will personally hand him over. Preferably with his case tied up in a little bow." She gave me a direct look. "But if we played any part in this, we owe it to the man that died. We have to figure out what happened. And I need your help."

# TEN

I had set an alarm for Saturday morning, but my fitful night's sleep ended far before any warning would come. I didn't want to dig myself any deeper into this potential scandal, but I couldn't see any other way. Sloan was right. I couldn't live with the uncertainty.

There was no way but forward, until we discovered the truth. My only hope was that we would find nothing unseemly, and I could go back to my safe, quiet life with a clear conscience.

In the afternoon I dressed in a white button-up and black pencil skirt, as instructed, and headed back to the parking lot of Westbrook Trading. Sloan was waiting for me in her car. There was only one other vehicle in the lot. I was curious what we were doing at the deserted office on a Saturday.

"Welcome to Westbrook," Sloan said. "There's someone I want you to meet."

As she let us into the hulking corporate office I noted

that we were wearing matching outfits, although my typical black flats were shown up by her shiny heels. But before I could question her, we turned a corner and came face to face with a petite curly-haired brunette. I startled slightly. She looked just as surprised to see us.

"Oh, it's just you," she said. "I'm in here after hours all the time, but it's still creepy when you're here all by yourself."

"I'd be creeped out *all* the time if I worked directly for Richard Westbrook," Sloan said. "Quinn, meet Hannah Porter. Richard's assistant and our inside man."

We exchanged greetings.

Hannah looked us over, humored. "What's with the Bobbsey twins thing?"

"She just likes to copy me." Sloan grinned, ignoring my scoff. "Quinn's helping me check into some things. And we could use your help."

"What do you need?"

"Access. Your boss is still keeping things from me, even though he hired me to consult for him. There are many things I need to take into consideration, including his personal finances. And he just doesn't seem to get it."

Hannah nodded knowingly. "He can be pretty stubborn."

"So could you do us a favor and give us access to his computer?"

Hannah tucked her thick mane behind one ear, looking wary.

Sloan continued. "I need to know the full picture before I can advise him. Something funny is going on. The company could be in trouble."

Hannah looked a little alarmed at her statement. "But you can't tell me exactly what you're checking into?"

Sloan shook her head. "Sorry. Still can't. But if it makes you feel better, the contract Richard signed gives me access to his information as a client. I can send you a copy. I'd just rather not have him fight it and try to hide things from me, against his own interests."

Hannah bit her lip, considering the request. Finally she shrugged. "Well, he did hire you. Okay. But this is just between us. And I'll need to watch."

"Better than that. You can help."

We followed Sloan down the hall to an expansive office with a large carved dark wood desk. One wall was mostly glass overlooking greenery to the side of the building.

Sloan settled into the chair behind the desk and started the computer. "First things first—you know the password to the computer?"

Hannah leaned over and typed in the code. I inched closer, feeling awkward about the invasion.

"We're in." Sloan looked to me. "Where would you start?"

"Um, email?"

"Sounds good to me." Sloan started his email client. It opened without prompting for a password.

We quickly skimmed emails in his office account. Nothing jumped out. A focus on communications between Richard and his brother indicated nothing noteworthy.

"So what exactly do they do here, anyway?" I asked Hannah while Sloan continued to scroll and click. "Money management, right?"

"Right. Some long-term investments. Retirements, that sort of thing. But the big money is in short-term investments. Trying to beat the market. It's like a game to them. A very intense, high-stakes game."

I checked out the room. Nothing out of place, the office was spare but expensive. The traditional nailhead trimmed leather armchairs and heavy woods contrasted with the modern glass-walled building. I noted a lack of photos or anything remotely personal-looking.

"Meetings, instructions, appointments." Sloan sounded bored. "This would take forever to go through, but so far it just looks like mundane office stuff. I doubt anything funny would come through there anyway. Does he have a personal email?"

"Actually, yes," Hannah said. "But I don't think he even knows I've seen it."

Sloan offered the mouse and Hannah maneuvered to a list of bookmarks in his internet browser. Once again it instantly logged in and an inbox appeared on the screen. One new email was waiting. The subject line was blank.

Sloan clicked to open. The email contained only two

lines. *I am getting impatient. You will not like me impatient.* There was no signature.

"Well, that's a little ominous. Any idea who that is?"

Hannah shook her head. "The username looks like random letters. Never seen it before."

Sloan marked the email as new to make it appear unopened and continued into the older emails in the account. Old reservation confirmations and receipts. Some email marketing. Very little personal communication, except for a few emails back and forth about commitments with what looked to be extended family members. None from any obvious spouse.

But several emails from his son, all signed 'B'. They all addressed him as Dad and began with some basic pleasantries, before begging for substantial sums of money.

"I knew it," Hannah suddenly exclaimed from behind us.

Sloan and I looked up in surprise.

She was gaping at the screen. "He's always implied that he's living off some giant trust fund or something. But really he's just mooching off his father every chance he gets."

Sloan pointed to the screen. "I take it you know his son?"

Hannah raised her eyebrows. "I didn't mention that? *Blaine* is Richard's son."

Sloan and I exchanged a look before she spoke. "Blaine, your boyfriend? The bartender?"

87

"Yes, that Blaine. That's how we met. I've been working for Richard for a while, unfortunately. Blaine eventually came along and laid on the charm."

"Yeah, you left that part out," Sloan said, musing.

I leaned into the conversation. "If Richard is his father, why is he bartending? Seems like an odd choice."

"He's always said he was taking a break, sort of 'finding himself' before he settled down into starting his own company or something. But really he's just a lazy twenty-six year-old freeloading off his parents."

Sloan grinned. "Well, it looks like his father has the same opinion. His responses here seem to get increasingly reluctant to hand over more dough."

"Good," Hannah said, indignant. "You know, I don't care that he doesn't actually have money. But he's been lying to me all this time. I thought he was a budding entrepreneur, just plotting his dream investment. No wonder he never wants to talk about his plans."

I let a small chuckle slip out at the thought. Both of them turned at the sound.

"Sorry, no offense," I said. "I just had trouble picturing him as any kind of business prodigy. But I don't know him at all."

"No, that's okay." Hannah looked between Sloan and I. "I take it you've met him, then. So did you guys check him out? What did you find?"

"We did," Sloan said. "And let's just say—if I were an investor, I would not put my money on Blaine turning out to be a good long-term investment, business or relationship-wise."

Hannah sighed, looking disappointed. "That's it. I'm dumping him."

Sloan quickly continued. "But we really don't have enough information yet. No real proof." She glanced quickly to me, her eyes narrowing with an idea before returning to Hannah. "Don't do anything just yet. Let us dig a little deeper first. Maybe he's just a big flirt for tips. Apparently he *is* broke, after all."

Hannah returned a reluctant smile and shook her head. "I don't know how exactly I can break up with my jerk of a boss's son without ramifications, anyway. I don't know what I was thinking."

"Can't help you there. Although he does have his charms." Sloan gave her a sympathetic smile and turned back to the computer screen. "In the meantime, let's see what else we can find out about Papa Moneybags. I saw bank names listed in his browser bookmarks. Can you get into those?"

Hannah nodded. "Everything is set to log in automatically. If you know the password to his computer, you basically know the password to it all."

"Not very security-minded, is he? He could use a little consulting on his data protection, too."

*Accessing his bank accounts?* I was beginning to be concerned with my participation in this little venture. "Um, is this legal?"

"We're sort of working in a couple of gray areas here," Sloan said. She looked to Hannah. "I assume you know how to get into these accounts because he has you access them on his behalf sometimes?"

Hannah nodded, looking just as concerned about the legality as I was.

"Then he's set a precedent that you're allowed to see them. You have a 'reasonable expectation' that you have permission. We aren't touching anything, just looking. Plus, like I said, his contract has clauses that give me permission to access his information if needed in the process of my inquiry. So I'd rather not advertise our access to him, but I'm not worried about it either."

I felt a little better, although I had no idea whether any of that were legally true. At least I hadn't physically done any prying so far.

Sloan logged into the first bank website listed. Two accounts appeared.

Hannah spoke up, sounding a little uncomfortable. "So, what is it you're looking for?"

"Anything unusual that explains some questionable incidents. There may be criminal activity occurring right under his nose." *Always as vague as possible, expertly avoiding outright lies.*

She clicked to access the first account. "Checking account. Not exactly empty, but I've seen the guy's house. I would expect a little more padding in his account to cover his overhead." She browsed through the history.

"Large credit card payments and regular ATM withdrawals, on top of what looks like the usual monthly expenses. Adds up to much more than the generous paychecks deposited. He's been transferring in chunks from his savings the last six months to stay afloat."

Sloan switched our view to the savings account and scrolled quickly through the history. Her eyebrows went up when she reached the end of the accessible data. "His savings sure have taken a hit from all the withdrawals. He used to transfer in a ton every month. Now it only flows out, and is dwindling fast."

"Maybe he's not the problem," I said. "Is he married?"

"Divorced," Hannah answered. "She dumped the selfish jerk years ago."

"Well, there were several banks on the list," I pointed out. "Maybe he's putting it somewhere else."

"Good point." Sloan logged out and moved on to the next bookmark. "Nope, this one's a credit card."

I looked over the numbers. "Whoa, a big credit card. Surely that can't be the balance."

"I think perhaps your boss has a bit of a debt problem," Sloan said. She turned to Hannah. "Did you know?"

She shook her head. "He acts like everything's fine. I thought he was rolling in it. He and Blaine both."

"Like father, like son," Sloan said. "Isn't that sweet."

She continued clicking through the list of financial bookmarks and we quickly skimmed the contents of each.

"Just more of the same," Sloan said. "He seems to like

cash-advances, despite the fact that they're one of the worst possible ways to get money. With his success, he can't be a stupid man."

Hannah looked skeptical. "He's a lot of things, but stupid is not one of them. As a businessman, I'd more likely describe him as *conniving*."

Sloan shrugged. "Then I don't get it."

She pulled her phone from her bag and snapped a picture of the screen showing one of the several high-balance credit card accounts.

"Okay, I think we're done here." Sloan turned to Hannah. "I really appreciate your help on this. I'd like to retain the option to return if needed. But please keep this little exploration between us. No need to poke the bear."

Hannah grinned. "Couldn't agree more."

# ELEVEN

Apparently the digital snooping was only Phase One of the day Sloan had planned. Our next stop was a dinner break. At this point I didn't even need to ask the venue. I was getting the feeling the ancient diner was a bit of an addiction to Sloan. She seemed most comfortable there.

I leaned back in my booth as I took a sip of my coffee. "So what's on the agenda for tonight?"

"We're back on Walter-watch," Sloan replied. "He's supposed to be going to a party, sans the wife. She's out of town for the weekend."

"Walter? Aren't we going to keep looking into Richard?" I lowered my voice to a whisper. "And the suspicious death?"

"Of course. I'm still figuring out our next moves on that front. But in the meantime I have to keep doing the job I was hired to do, or Richard'll get suspicious. We have to keep the suspect happy."

That made sense. "Any reason to suspect anything with Walter for tonight?"

Sloan shrugged. "Richard seems to think so, and told me I better be watching. He said the CEO in question won't be there, but there may be other women of suspicion. I still have my doubts. But I guess we'll see."

Before long, Dottie returned with our food. My mouth watered when she laid the still–bubbling chicken pot pies in front of us.

"Thanks, Dottie," Sloan said. "Is Sayid here? I'd like to introduce him to Quinn."

"Washing dishes tonight. I'll tell him to come out."

When Dottie walked away, I broke off a piece of crust, too impatient to wait for the filling to cool. It was delicious. Sloan used a spoon to smash in the top of her crust, letting out a savory steam.

"Yours looked so good last time I had to try it," she said. "I normally always eat breakfast here, no matter what time it is."

"Any particular reason?"

She paused for a moment, then shrugged. "I just like it." Her eyes were averted.

I was halfway through my meal when I noticed Sloan had put down her spoon and was smiling past me. Just then I sensed someone approaching from behind. When the male figure reached our table, I looked up—into the face of the young man from the bookstore coffee shop.

The one that had stared at me ominously until I found the mysterious note that started this entire adventure. I quickly swallowed my mouthful.

"Quinn, this is Sayid," Sloan said. "I believe you two haven't formally met."

His stoic face broke into a shy smile, revealing straight white teeth that contrasted against his dark hair and skin. He was handsome but young; I figured he couldn't be older than twenty.

"It's very nice to meet you, Quinn," he answered with just a hint of an accent. He offered his hand.

I shook it. "You, too."

Sloan was grinning. "So Sayid was doing me a favor the first time you saw him. He was supposed to make you a little on edge, just to mess with you. Kind of set the stage. I guess it must've worked."

Sayid's smile was sheepish. "Sorry about that."

I laughed, remembering my discomfort that day. "No problem."

"Sayid's father owns Joe's Diner," Sloan said. "He's studying engineering nearby, and helps out here part-time. He's ridiculously smart."

Sayid blushed a little.

Sloan smiled at him. "You basically helped me interview Quinn here, and now she's on board. She's going to be helping me."

"No promises," I interjected.

"Okay, whatever," Sloan replied breezily.

I thought of the name of the diner and looked up at Sayid, a little skeptical. "So is your father *Joe*?"

I caught his quick glance to Sloan before he shook his head. "Joe died a long time ago. My father bought this many years ago."

"And Sayid's been helping here ever since," Sloan added. "He makes a mean French toast. And you have to try his little chocolate coconut peanut-butter balls, they are to die for. Off-the-menu specialty."

I smiled at the serious young man. "You had me at coconut. I'll have to try it. And I like it here. Homey."

"Happy to hear that." Sayid reddened a little again. "I'd better get back to work. But I know how persistent she can be, so I'm sure I'll see you again. Nice to meet you."

I returned his farewell, and he headed back to the kitchen.

I picked up my spoon to finish dinner. "Well that clears that up. What about the scary guy on the train?"

Sloan grinned broadly. "Funny you should ask that." She raised her voice a bit. "Leo, care to make yourself known?"

A loud sigh in response came from the booth behind Sloan. A figure in a worn baseball cap shook his head and began to slide out of the seat. A moment later a young Asian face hidden under the dark hat and thick-framed glasses peered at us from the head of the table. A beige trench coat hung in folds around him, giving the impression of a child playing dress-up.

The man glared at Sloan and removed the baseball cap. Dark hair tucked underneath fell across his forehead and around his ears. He shook off the overcoat, revealing dark jeans and a hoodie zipped over several layers. When he pulled off his glasses and tossed them on the table, the same mischievous eyes that had haunted me met mine once again. I could only stare back, completely lost.

Sloan looked to me, humor in her eyes. "I planned a little reunion. Let you get to know the crew." She motioned toward the newcomer. "So this is Leo, my favorite hacker."

He scowled and gave her another glare before shoving himself into the seat beside her.

"Sorry," she said, shifting over for him. "He doesn't like when I use that term in public. He's a 'computer expert.'" Her mocking tone was emphasized with air quotes.

Leo sighed in annoyance and turned his attention to me. He reached his hand across. "Hi."

"Quinn," I said, returning the grasp. "Nice to meet you."

For the first time he lost some of his intensity, and up close I realized he was probably older than I had first assumed. The outfit was still youthful, but his face had the kind of still confidence that can only come with age. His strong jaw and cheekbones gave a chiseled effect to his face. I figured early thirties.

I looked between them, waiting for an explanation of the unusual entrance. "So? What was that about?"

Sloan spoke up. "I think that was a clear demonstration that Leo should stick to what he knows and leave the subterfuge to me. In real life, anyway."

"Hey, it's not easy hiding a face like this," he scoffed. "It's not my fault my exceptionally handsome face can't be disguised."

"It is more difficult, I'll give you that," Sloan agreed. "With your bone structure, I'd have to hook you up with some wax in your cheek to change the whole shape of your face. Girls are a lot easier."

"Well, I had a few extra minutes so I thought I'd give it a try." Leo looked defeated but amused. "Probably should've at least borrowed a coat that fit. I didn't think you paid me any attention."

"I know." Sloan returned a playful smugness. "Because that's how it's done."

He turned to me and his dark eyes took me in with curiosity. "So what has Sloan here dragged you into? I feel the need to warn you, this girl can only mean trouble."

Sloan scoffed. "And when have I ever gotten you in trouble?"

"That isn't the question. The question is—when do you put me in a position to get in trouble? All the time. I just happen to be good at not getting caught."

"Whatever. You live for the subversion."

Leo conceded with a shrug and returned his attention to me.

98

"Thanks for the warning," I said. "But I'm just helping out a little."

Sloan picked up her spoon to resume eating. "Leo can help us, too. I gave him whatever Westbrook Trading documents we were able to get, because I don't fully understand what we're dealing with." She looked to Leo. "So what can you tell us about the deal they're working on? Anything illegal?"

His eyes narrowed, considering. "Not *definitely* illegal. It's supposedly focused on Westbrook's exclusive use of software made by Quandom. Maybe some hardware too. Hard to tell exactly. But I think there's more than just a simple exchange of goods going on. Everything is too vague to be completely legit."

I tried to think of what I knew about Quandom Corp. They had been surprisingly vague with me about their business so far as well. All I had gathered is that they manufactured some tech equipment including fiber optic cables—but I got the feeling their real interest was in R&D. "I didn't know they were making anything for use in the stock market."

"That's the secret part. I think they've developed algorithms to increase the processing speed of automated decisions. And possibly the speed of transmitting those trades." He lowered his voice a little. "And considering the connections the tech company has, I have a feeling we're talking about some underground super-speed technology no one else is using yet. Except maybe the military."

"What makes you say that?" Sloan asked.

"Like a lot of the companies around here, they're primarily a military contractor. But they seem to be hiding it. Let's just say most of their income comes from what I believe are really shell corporations for the intelligence community. If so, that would explain why this deal is supposedly so top secret."

I was lost. "What do you mean?"

"Reading between the lines, I'd say Quandom is probably letting this fairly small and local investment firm access this technology, hoping it won't attract attention." His eyes began to twinkle. "And so their usual customer doesn't realize they're letting someone else in on some truly sweet, so-far unseen technology. I'd love to get my hands on whatever they're dealing with."

"Okay, so their stuff is unusually fast," Sloan said. "What would this extra speed get Westbrook Trading?"

"A whole different level of playing field. Heck, a new game." Leo's whole face lit up. "They could enter the realm of high-frequency trading. And win huge, if their technology is ahead of the competition. It's all a speed game."

The term sounded vaguely familiar, but I was unclear what exactly it meant. "High-frequency trading? Is that just faster?"

"Compared to what they were doing before, it's like going from regular physics to quantum physics. When you go down to such a tiny, incomprehensible scale, all the old rules go out the window. They use algorithms and high-speed connections to conduct lightning-fast trades."

Leo became more animated as he explained, his eyes wide with excitement. "We're talking nanoseconds—a billionth of a second. The idea is to make tiny bits of profit off each trade, multiplied by thousands of trades a second. Massive money can be made. Automatically, in the blink of an eye."

I had trouble wrapping my head around numbers like that. "So you think this other company is going to supply the software that allows them to trade at those speeds?"

"Like I said, probably a combination of super-fast processing with high-speed transmission capabilities. If they got set up next to the physical exchange, the computers would conduct all the trading for them, without them having to do a thing." He leaned back into his seat, striking a relaxed pose. "They could just sit back, hundreds of miles away, and watch the money pile up in their accounts."

Sloan looked just as awed. "So this sort of thing is completely legal?"

Leo shrugged. "Investors like this make absolutely no contribution to the world, just make the whole stock market at risk for collapse if something goes haywire. But these guys make a lot of money, so you can imagine the kind of influence they have."

The whole system was bizarre to me. What was the point, besides greed?

"There's talk of putting speed limits on the market," he continued. "But good luck enforcing that. My guess is these investment guys would only have use of this technology for a short window of time. Before long someone's going to get wind of it and want their piece. But they can certainly make a pretty penny in the meantime."

Dottie approached the table, coffee in hand. She looked to Leo. "We were wondering what you were up this time, but you know I don't ask questions when you guys are playing dress-up." She tried unsuccessfully to hide a laugh. "Not sure who you thought you were fooling, though. Want some coffee?"

"Thanks, but I actually need to head out." Leo turned back to us. "Did that help?"

"Absolutely," Sloan replied. "Go. Run off to your girlfriend. Tell her I said hi."

He slid out of the booth, grinning, and Dottie wordlessly poured each of us a cup and disappeared.

"Learn new things everyday," Sloan said, reaching for the sugar.

"Yeah, I'm going to need to let that simmer for a bit."

"Agreed. So listen, there's one other thing you need to know about tonight. That party we're going to? We're not exactly going as guests. Richard called in a favor to get me on as the help. And I'm going to be showing up with a friend."

*That explains our matching outfits.* "The help? What, like caterers?"

"Sort of. We won't have to actually do anything. Just walk around offering hors d'oeuvres. This way we can split up and keep an eye on Walter at all times without having to mingle. You think you can handle smiling and holding a tray?"

I smiled. "I think I can do that."

# TWELVE

At least by being fake caterers, we didn't have to show up early for all the prep work. As soon as we arrived, we were handed platters with tiny morsels and hustled out of the kitchen by a harried catering manager. Thankfully, neither she nor the party host had asked any questions about our presence.

We surveyed the great room before splitting up. No sign of our target.

Sloan leaned in to whisper. "You know what's disturbing about getting set up for a gig like this? Richard must've implied a reason for wanting to help me get a catering job. And I sincerely doubt he does anything out of the goodness of his heart. I didn't even want to look the host in the eye."

"Oh, gross. You're right."

"At least Richard won't be here. Keep an eye out for his brother."

We split up. I stayed in the main room while Sloan

wandered into the next. I slowly meandered through the party, a mild polite smile plastered on my face. It appeared to be mainly professionals quietly chatting, probably more networking than anything else. Within minutes I recognized Walter entering the low-key gathering. He said hello to a couple of acquaintances on his way to the small bar.

From across the room, I noticed one of the guests also seemed keenly interested in Walter's arrival. The attractive middle-aged blonde watched him from afar for a few moments before edging near. When he turned away from the bar, she quickly brushed past him, causing a collision. His drink splashed onto both of them.

Walter apologized for his clumsiness and fetched her cocktail napkins for the small spot of soda left on her dress. I felt certain the incident had been on purpose. She blotted at the stain and they moved to the side of the room as the woman kept him in conversation. I had to remind myself to keep moving and not stare.

But the vigilance was at least successful in diverting attention from my itchy head. Sloan had talked me into wearing a wig for the event. The light-brown shoulder-length bob would reduce the chances that I would be recognized on a future surveillance, she argued. I topped it off with some large hoop earrings I would never normally wear. And I had to admit, being in disguise was a little liberating.

Like most food service help, the guests paid me little attention. So I felt confident no one noticed when I snapped several photos of the pair using the pinhole camera Sloan had installed in my blouse. The button hiding the camera was slightly different from the rest, but again, there was almost zero chance anyone would notice. I simply pushed a button hidden in my side to take the shots.

The woman was pretty blatantly flirting with Walter. It was mostly a lot of upper arm touches and eyelash batting. *Maybe this is the other woman we're looking for.* But I couldn't quite get a read on Walter. He was very polite and engaged, but didn't really give back the same vibe.

A perky voice spoke up from behind. "I think they need some salmon puffs in the next room." When I turned, it took me a moment to re-register that the bubbly blonde speaking to me was Sloan. "I'll take over for you in here," she said, her eyes roving to the targets before giving me a sly smile.

I nodded and left without a word. As I circulated through the formal living areas, I wondered about the relationship of the pair. I hadn't perceived any kind of intimacy. If something was going on between them, it seemed new.

The party dragged on. Two trays of hors d'oeuvres later, I was beginning to get anxious about what Sloan had found. It was time to discover something juicy. Suddenly Sloan appeared and headed straight for me. She grabbed the tray from my hands and laid it on a nearby table.

"They're leaving together," Sloan whispered. "She asked him for a ride home. Go out through the back and see what you can find."

"You're not coming?"

"It'll be suspicious if we both disappear. I'll try to get out soon. I trust you."

I hesitated only a moment. When Sloan nodded toward a back hallway, I casually strolled out of sight and exited onto the back patio. As I rounded the side of the house, I spotted the pair and hid behind manicured shrubbery. Walter helped the woman into his passenger seat.

Once they were on the road, I made a run for my car down the street.

\*\*\*

We still hadn't officially gone over how to tail properly. I just pictured scenes from movies and television, where people in dark sunglasses casually weaved through traffic, following at a distance. It didn't look that hard.

I couldn't use sunglasses at night, but I stayed back what I thought was a reasonable distance and kept my eye on the tan Infiniti. While we drove I removed my earrings and twisted my fake hair into a clip to change my appearance a bit. It felt very professional spy-like.

What did not feel professional spy-like was losing the target during a simple tail. As we approached a large intersection, Walter suddenly moved to the far right, crossing three lanes of traffic at the last second. *Does he know I'm back here?* It didn't seem likely. But I couldn't possibly copy his maneuver without raising suspicion, especially in the light traffic, so I was forced to continue on through the intersection. Walter turned and disappeared.

I took a right at the next intersection, hoping it would head toward a crossing. This section of town, mostly suburban commercial, was not set in a grid pattern. As the road began to wind in the opposite direction, I felt a panic forming. I had probably lost them. *This could be the crucial moment, and Sloan trusted me with it.* I couldn't let her down like that.

Luckily, I was generally good with directions. Even though the area was unfamiliar, I had a pretty good feel for where I was in relation to where I thought the Infiniti was headed. When an opportunistic turn appeared, I took it and raced through several side streets, trying to get back on track. If they had turned off the main road already, I was sunk. I would never find them in the maze of neighborhoods surrounding us.

Finally, I found the original thoroughfare he had taken. I turned left onto the road and sped, trying to catch up. No sign of them. Just as I was ready to call Sloan in defeat, I saw taillights in the distance ahead. A minute later they turned off the main drag, and I was relieved to see the car could be a match. I zoomed ahead to follow again.

Whether it was them or not, I would definitely have to keep my distance as we rolled through the residential area. The car wound its way through a nice middle-class neighborhood and slowed in front of a two-story red-brick home. I made note of the address but had no choice but to continue past. I took the next turn and parked, hidden by the house on the corner. Once again I was grateful for my car's stealth-mode engine that cut off silently.

It was at this point I realized I wasn't sure what Sloan expected me to do, and I didn't have long to consider. I disabled the door light and slipped out of the car, camera in hand. The neighborhood was very quiet, settling into bedtimes. I peeked around the corner of the house and was able to catch a glimpse of the pair walking away from the car. Target confirmed. Only a few houses down.

I knew if he went into the house, presumably the mystery woman's, it would be crucial to get a shot of it. Moving to the backyard, I found my path unencumbered by fences and raced across several lawns through the shadows, praying there were no motion-activated lights along the way.

I emerged along the side of the red brick house just as they stepped onto the low front porch. A clear view. I tried to slow my breathing to ensure I wouldn't be heard.

They chatted a moment before the woman unlocked the door. I couldn't quite make out what they were saying. Just a few friendly laughs from the woman. She pushed the front door open and turned back to Walter. He offered his hand, as if to shake with a business acquaintance. The woman returned his grasp. *Maybe there's nothing going on here. Oh—wait.* The woman reached up his arm with her other hand. It no longer looked so businesslike. I couldn't see Walter's face. I began snapping photos.

The woman stepped closer to Walter, now speaking so softly that the only evidence was the moving of her lips. Her face moved dangerously close to his. He didn't seem to respond. Finally he took a step back, shaking his head. He gently but gingerly removed her hand from his arm.

I felt a vague affection for Walter as I watched the woman's expression turn from sultry to offended. He waited for her to retreat into her house, then headed for his car. I made sure to capture the entire scene on the camera. Point one for Walter's integrity.

As he climbed into the Infiniti, I realized my job wasn't quite over. He was my responsibility until he was tucked safely in for the night. I turned on my heel and sprinted back to my car, grateful I had recently reintroduced my running routine. I would need to be in shape to handle this hobby.

*Was this a hobby?* Maybe more of an addiction.

# THIRTEEN

Except for his abrupt lane-changing earlier, which may have been due to a distracted passenger giving directions, Walter drove nothing like his brother. I followed him effortlessly for a few miles to another neighborhood, this time of slightly grander homes. I felt certain he was headed home. I stayed down the street when he pulled into the garage of a large two-story traditional and lights flicked on in the darkened house.

Unsure where to go next, I tried Sloan's phone. No answer. I figured she could be still handing out hors d'oeuvres, working her cover. Lights came on upstairs in Walter's house. *Headed to bed. Maybe I should just do the same?* Giving it just a few minutes, I pulled out the camera to review the photographs and consider what I had seen so far.

I looked through the collection, cringing every time headlights passed and illuminated me sitting suspiciously in my parked car. *So far everything checks out on this guy.*

*I should get out of here.* I returned the camera to its case and placed it within reach in the back.

Suddenly my passenger door swung open and a hooded figure in black launched themselves into the seat. My heart stopped for a moment. With the overhead light disabled I couldn't see their face.

But the panic only lasted a moment as I quickly placed the bare leg and peep toe heels. *Sloan.* She pulled down the hood of her sweatshirt and faced me, grinning.

"Don't you keep your doors locked?" she said. "Rule number one: always protect yourself. I could've been anyone."

I gaped at her, my pulse still jagged. "What are you doing here? How did you find me?"

She shrugged. "I put a tracker on your car."

"You what?"

She pulled down the passenger visor and began fixing her ruffled hair in the lighted mirror. "I told you, protection is a priority. I don't want to send you out on something without being able to find you. Especially with you as a beginner. I'm responsible for you, newbie."

Well, technically I *was* working for her, although we hadn't actually discussed any pay at that point. Maybe it did make sense for her to have tabs on me. I could feel safer. It was just the secrecy of it that was so jarring.

Then it occurred to me. "Wait, if you had a tracker this whole time, why didn't you just use it on our guy? I could've followed him without all the stress. I almost lost him."

"You want to learn the skills, right?" Sloan gave her usual confident nonchalance. "You won't always be able to have technology do the work. Have to learn to do it old school."

*Hmph.* She was right, but all the toying with me was a little irksome. You never knew what to expect with this girl. I handed over the camera without a word, letting my best frustrated face do the talking.

Sloan ignored my expression and glanced quickly through the photos I had taken. Then she laid the camera in her lap and looked to me with a mock frown. "You still mad at me?"

I had to laugh at her exaggeration. "It does make sense for safety reasons. But you sure like to keep things secret until the last second, huh?"

Sloan grinned. "Of course. What fun is telling everything up front? Surprises are the best."

"Interesting." I gave her a mischievous look. "I'll have to remember that."

"Oh, no. It's only fun when *I* do it."

Both of our eyes flicked to the house down the street as we perceived a change. The upstairs lights had turned off. Walter had gone to bed.

Sloan turned back to me and held up the camera. "This is great work. You can clearly see there was some kind of opportunity, and Walter didn't go for it. Could you hear what was going on?"

I shook my head. "Too far away."

"And no chance you were seen, right?"

"No way."

"Then I'm wondering what we're doing here," Sloan mused. "So far he's a nice guy who takes out his wife, gives women rides home, and turns them down on their doorstep. What am I missing?"

"And you didn't see them first talk at the party. I'm not sure if he already knew her or not—but I swear she made a beeline for him when he walked in, and purposefully created a reason to talk to him."

Sloan shook her head in disbelief. "That would seem reasonable if he were someone else. Younger, sexier, more charming. Or really rich. He looks like he's doing well, but certainly not women-throwing-themselves-at-him wealthy. I really don't get it."

"I'm with you." I looked toward Walter's darkened house. "I assume there's nothing else on the agenda for tonight?"

"Looks like that's it. But if Blaine is working at the bar tomorrow, I'd like to have another chat with him." Sloan grinned. "Now that we know he's Richard's son, we can try to squeeze some information out of him, too. Two birds with one stone."

She opened the car door to exit. "See you tom—wait."

I followed her eyes toward Walter's house. The light had returned upstairs. She pulled the door shut again.

I glanced at Sloan. "Midnight snack?"

"Probably something like that. Let's just wait to be sure."

We watched in silence. More lights appeared. A few minutes later the garage door opened and Walter's car began backing down the driveway. I looked at Sloan in surprise.

She narrowed her eyes, dubious. "Don't tell me he has a booty call. Although the wife is out of town . . ."

I shook my head. "I don't buy that."

"Let's find out." She opened her door again as Walter's car began down the street. "We'll both follow. It'll be easier with two cars. Stay way back and I'll tell you when to take the lead."

She slipped out of the car and ran, pulling her hood back over her head. I had apparently never even noticed her vehicle pulling in down the street behind me. Her car took off down the road and I fell in far behind them.

*** 

On the drive I began to learn some tips for a multi-car tail. Sloan would turn away from the target and I would move in closer. Then we would switch positions again, never getting too close. Repeat as necessary. I believed I could get the hang of it.

When we pulled onto a smaller secondary road, I knew we had to be nearing our destination. The commercial street was lined with dark restaurants and shops, all long-closed at this time of night.

Sloan's voice sounded in my ear. "I'm going to pull off up here. Follow him into wherever he's going."

I saw her taillights ahead turn onto a side street and increased my speed slightly. A minute later the Infiniti pulled off as well. I yanked the wheel and entered the gas station next door to avoid obviously following him into the mostly empty lot.

Walter pulled up to the unlit front door of a two-story white stucco building and hustled inside. Only the sign out front was illuminated, indicating the place was an Italian restaurant. *Villa Coppola.* Clearly looked closed. I couldn't possibly follow him inside at this point, especially still wearing my catering outfit. So I watched, intrigued.

Walter quickly reappeared in the doorway with another figure. The hefty man was slumped over, an arm over Walter's shoulders. *Richard.*

Walter moved carefully to the other side of his car, clearly straining under the weight of his swaying older brother. He managed to open the door and Richard flopped unceremoniously into the seat. Walter tucked him in and returned to his seat behind the wheel.

Sloan was still connected by phone but had stayed quiet while I figured out the scene. As Walter pulled out of the lot, I caught her up and let her know his direction. She moved back into position for the return tail.

Meanwhile I scanned the lot for Richard's car. Sure enough, his red Porsche was sitting in the front row.

"So 'ol Dick was sloppy drunk, huh?" Sloan said.

"Wonder how often his little brother has to come rescue him."

"Don't know. But with all his debt, drinking could be either the cause or the result of his money problems. Or possibly both."

"Good point. We should check out the charges on his credit cards more closely. Maybe our client has all sorts of vices."

The case and client were definitely curious. "So what's he doing being so nosy about his brother's private business then?"

"That's a *very* good question."

# FOURTEEN

I slept late Sunday morning, exhausted from the long day of snooping. Once Walter had deposited his brother at his house and it was clear he was headed home again, we had finally called it a night. I had the afternoon free before we would meet up just as Blaine's bartending shift started downtown.

I continued my new routine of a workout and finalizing preparation for my research study. I only had two more weeks before my free time would be tied up with data collection and then analyzation. And I hadn't exactly been focused on it thus far.

No disguises were required that night. We had agreed I would play only an ancillary role in this interview. Sloan figured that Blaine would be more candid, and more forward, if she appeared to be alone. I had no problem with taking a backseat. I had yet to actively, purposefully perpetrate a deception, except for a little white lie to get out of a jam, and I just wasn't sure I was ready to yet.

Instead I would simply listen and record their conversation, by combining my hearing device streaming with a recording program on my phone. My presence wasn't truly necessary, but Sloan wanted the backup and a second take on the situation. I was happy to stay involved.

At the appointed time that evening, I entered the restaurant and headed toward the back. But just before I reached the bar, I followed Sloan's directions and took a right turn.

The alcove I found myself in separated the sunny restaurant in front from the dimly-lit back bar area. Small rectangular cutouts in the walls leading to the restrooms allowed slivered views into both sections. Positioned next to the bar but hidden from view, I would be able to stay connected to Sloan's conversation. The plan didn't require Blaine ever even knowing I was there.

I pulled out my phone and readied it. A quick peek into the bar informed me that Blaine was on duty. A moment later Sloan appeared around the corner. Wordlessly she checked her hair in the hall mirror, gave me a quick wink, and continued on into the back.

The sound levels increased in my ears as I tuned into her path toward the bar. Blaine's voice didn't take long to materialize. His greeting indicated he clearly remembered her.

Sloan giggled. "I'm supposed to be meeting someone, but I'm not sure if they're coming."

"Well, just my luck. I'll be glad to keep you company."

I settled in for a long, flirtatious back and forth. I knew Sloan wouldn't just jump right in; she would need to warm him up first, create a bond between them. Then she'd likely be able to ask him anything. Once again I listened closely to learn how she handled things. She took her time, resuming the conversation in between his service of other customers.

Blaine eventually got back around to what I believed was his agenda. "So listen, you said you don't have a boyfriend? How is that even possible?"

I took another peek through the wall opening. Blaine was leaning across the bar toward Sloan, elbows resting on the bar top. She had his full attention.

Sloan gave him a shrug with a coy look in return. "No guys have been holding my interest, I guess."

Blaine was still leaning across the bar, enraptured, when I moved away from the window.

"So you're available, then?"

"Well, I didn't say all that," Sloan replied. "I am attracted to ambition, though. And money doesn't hurt."

"Well hey, you wouldn't believe it, but I'm loaded with both."

Sloan laughed good-naturedly. "You're right, I wouldn't believe it."

"Okay, well maybe not this second. But my dad is. And he's grooming me to take over one day."

"So is this just a second job then?"

"Nah, but I won't be here much longer. My dad's cutting me off. I have to go work for the family company and 'earn for myself.' So unfortunately, no more chatting with beautiful ladies like you for a living."

"Ouch," Sloan said. "But maybe the job's not so bad. You said you'll be in charge one day. That's kinda hot. So what does your father do?"

"The company is Westbrook Trading. Ever heard of it?"

"Um, maybe. Investing, I'm guessing?"

"Exactly," Blaine replied. "All kinds of boring financial stuff. My dad's the president. Well, co-president, with his brother. So I should be ranking up pretty good in no time. Never really wanted to be one of the suits, but I guess learning to be their boss could be alright."

"So he's sending you straight to the top? That sounds like a pretty good gig."

"Nah. Have to start at the bottom." His voice became mocking. "Just like everybody else."

"I take it you don't know much about investments, then?"

"Know it's a total snooze. But the money's off the hook. And about to get really ridiculous."

Sloan returned a playful skepticism. "Why, because you're getting into the game?"

"No, because there's a deal in play. Top secret."

"I'm intrigued. Do tell."

There was a brief pause that I interpreted as hesitation. I held my breath, hoping he would reveal something that was, in fact, intriguing.

Finally he spoke. "Let's just say—if this goes through, we won't be doing investments the hard way anymore. We'll finally be able to compete with the big dogs."

"Sounds impressive. But you're only making me more interested." Sloan's voice was quiet but emphatic. "You have to tell me the secret."

Another hesitation. Clearly Blaine was fighting his need to protect his future company with his desire to impress Sloan.

Sloan won.

"Seriously, this can't get out. I'm not even supposed to know about it."

"Our little secret," Sloan replied coyly.

"Okay, fine. We're about to get some kind of advantage. All I know is a crap-ton of money can be made by being faster than the other guys. And soon we'll be one of the fastest. Maybe *the* fastest."

So much for a revelation. All we've turned up so far is a rehash of everything we had already figured out.

"Wow, that sounds complicated, and sexy." Sloan's voice dripped with faked admiration. "I guess you're getting into the game just in time, then."

"Yeah, exactly. As long as everything goes through." Blaine's voice fell a little, his bravado slipping. "But it's not a done deal yet. For some reason my lame uncle is holding everything up."

My ears pricked up, suddenly riveted.

Sloan played it cool. "Your uncle, the co-president? Why would he do that?"

"Who knows. Afraid of being successful? He always was a wimp. All I know is he says he's gonna block the deal. As if he wouldn't get massively rich from it like the rest of us. Hang on a sec."

The conversation went dead for a moment, and I assumed Blaine needed to serve customers out of their vicinity. As we approached dinner time, the bar would only get more crowded and our ability to extract information would disappear. Our time was limited.

Blaine's voice reappeared. "Ok, sorry. Need another drink?"

"No thanks," Sloan replied. "So what's this titan-of-industry dad of yours like? You want to be just like him?"

"God no. We couldn't be more different. But he's rich, I definitely admire that."

Sloan laughed.

"Actually, you could meet him," Blaine continued. "He's supposed to be coming here for dinner tonight."

I froze.

"No way. He's coming here now?"

"Probably be here soon. He likes to come show his support for my choices by treating me like the rest of his help."

I didn't hear what was said after that, as my adrenaline spiked through the roof. *We can't let Richard see her talking to his son.* We were out of time.

126

I rushed to the cutout windows in the alcove and peeked out. The bar area looked clear. I turned and peered into the restaurant out front. Nothing again. I watched for a moment, thinking, as I tried to get my breathing under control. Until the front door swung open and Richard waltzed in.

*He'll figure out Sloan is investigating him.* The suspicion of a possible hit-for-hire user was the last thing we needed. I had to get her out of there. But I didn't know how to do it fast enough without arousing suspicion of a different sort.

Richard stepped to the side of the entry with his phone, finishing a conversation. *That'll buy us a little time.*

Suddenly I had an idea. A bizarre idea I wouldn't have even considered only a week ago. Without stopping to think it through, I gave myself a quick check in the mirror and hurried around the corner into the bar.

# FIFTEEN

Blaine was leaning across the bar again. He shifted back subtly when he spotted me heading toward them. "Hey, isn't that your friend?"

Sloan swiveled around on her barstool just as I approached. Her gaze met mine inquisitively.

Before she could speak, I reached to grab the back of her head and swooped in, my lips pressing brusquely against hers in one swift movement. She tensed in surprise momentarily but quickly recovered, softening as our lips touched. Her mouth was softer than I was used to. Gentler. The din of the bar quieted a little as our show was observed.

I pulled away slowly, locking eyes with Sloan and putting on my most confident face. "Hi," I said flirtatiously.

"Hi yourself." There was a mischievous twinkle in her eye.

I looked over at her now-gaping companion.

"Whoa, sorry," Blaine said, looking back and forth between us. He held up his hands in surrender. "I had no idea."

"No problem." I turned back to Sloan. "We should go. Now."

"Sure." She hopped from her stool and looked back at Blaine with a smug smile. "Good to see you."

He raised a beer in salute as we strode away, hand-in-hand. He was still watching when I led Sloan through the back door and out of the path of Richard. The perplexed look on his face was worth the entire scene.

We were practically running by the time we got to the car. We threw ourselves into the seats and she turned to me, eyes bright.

"What the hell was that!"

***

We found refuge in the parking lot down the street. I couldn't keep the grin off my face as I parked next to Sloan's car and turned to face her. She was staring at me, impatient. We both instantly burst out laughing.

"Seriously," she began. "What was that about?"

"Richard was about to come in and catch you talking to Blaine. I had to get you out of there quickly or he would figure things out."

"So you decided to play the lover card? What made you think of that?"

"It was your idea." I felt my face turning red as the scene replayed in my head. "You said once that playing the girlfriend could make for an easy exit. I'd say you were right."

Sloan seemed to think back to the conversation. "Well, you were brilliant, coming up with that on the spot. I think you're a natural at this."

I did feel pretty proud of myself. "Thanks."

She gave me a devious grin. "And not a bad kisser, either."

My face flamed to max this time. I flashed her a mock-haughty look. "Don't go getting any ideas."

Sloan gave a faux-shocked face in return, leading to another laughing fit from both of us.

I finally cleared my throat, trying to get back on track. "Well it was worth it, because we now know at least one lie the client has told. Richard said his brother was the one pushing for a deal, and that's why he wanted him checked out, right?"

"Exactly. That's the reason he gave for hiring me. To make sure Walter didn't have any ulterior motives. Now that we know Walter is actually the holdout on the deal, I'm wondering if Richard is really the one with the hidden agenda. And he just needed a plausible excuse to have me investigate Walter. Maybe he actually *wants* to catch him in the act."

"But why? Walter seems like a stand-up guy, and so far shows no signs of any affair."

Sloan looked just as confused. "I don't know. But we're going to need to keep an eye on both of them. Richard is looking for something. And now I'm just as interested in the *why* as the *what*."

\*\*\*

As if our discoveries of lies and secret motives weren't enough complication in my life, I got hit with a double whammy at work the next day. Because my relatively peaceful existence at the office turned into the Hunger Games by comparison. I thought the subtle derisive comments of my colleague peppered throughout the day were enough. I wasn't prepared for the coming onslaught.

"Okay, gather round," my boss announced as she burst into our little room at lunch. It was always just the two of us in there, so it wasn't much of a circle. We gave her our rapt attention.

"I have an important announcement. As you know, we sometimes take on fourth-year students following graduation. This year, we hope to do the same—but we will only have room for one. So if you're interested in the position, you'll have the chance to compete."

*This place would be my dream job.* Landing a position like this straight out of school would help set up the rest of my career. My ears perked up further as she continued.

"We know how you perform on the job, and I'm happy to say that so far we are pleased with both of you. So we're going to have you compete via presentation. Two weeks from today, each of you will present your dissertation projects to the rest of the faculty. We're looking to see your knowledge, poise, and overall professionalism. We'll review your performance and determine if we will be making an offer to one of you."

That didn't sound too bad. A fair appraisal of our work and research. Although it could possibly put a crimp in my sleuthing hobby, just as things were heating up.

Before I could finish processing, Grant jumped in. "Well, seeing as Quinn's my senior, and she was here before I was, I think I'll have a little trouble competing." He made a show of placing a hand to his chest, in an I'm-so-moved gesture. His puckered lips added an extra touch. "I respect and admire her and would never want to take *anything* that belongs to her."

Respect and admire? *Please*. And I'm only a year older than him.

He continued. "But I agree that a little competition can bring out the best in people. I certainly learned that in my years on the street, when you had to fight and scrap for everything to stay alive. You could never take anything for granted. So it taught me to be extremely determined and do what it takes."

I had serious doubts that competition to stay alive on the streets brought out the best in people. I suspected it frequently brought out something more like the most savage.

"That's very moving, Grant." Dr. Seymore's face was admiring. "I'm sure you'll have a unique take on it. And you, Quinn?"

*Yeah, moving alright. My lunch.* "Absolutely. Looking forward to it."

Dr. Seymore nodded with approval and stood to go.

"Let the best man win," Grant called after her. Once the door was closed, he turned to me, his false sincerity abandoned. "But just so you know, I'd do anything to win that position. Anything."

Now that, I believed. Which is why I was now very, very nervous.

# SIXTEEN

Sloan slid into her seat at our corner table. "Well, this place is cozy."

Indeed it was. The Italian restaurant from the other night, not much to look at from the outside, was warm and inviting in the main dining room. Fashioned from an old Spanish-style house, the place was softly lit by sconces that gave a soothing glow to the casually elegant ambiance.

I nodded in agreement. "I especially like the mural. It's a nice touch." The walls behind us were covered in floor-to-ceiling murals of an Italian cityscape. It appeared hand-painted and was quite vivid.

But we were here to take in more than just the scenery. So far it didn't exactly seem like the kind of establishment where one would come to get loaded. Intimate couples and small families at the surrounding tables were enjoying quiet dinners. I hadn't even seen a bar anywhere.

After a quick browse of the menu, I selected a simple

wine from the extensive list and relaxed into my seat. I was happy to finally have some down time. As expected, work had become infinitely more unpleasant working alongside my fellow intern since the announcement the day before. It was going to be a long two weeks.

"This is a nice break from the usual," I said. "So we don't need to worry about our target tonight? Whichever one that is."

Sloan put her menu down. "Both brothers are at the funeral. Showing support for their colleague. We're on our own for a few hours."

A waiter appeared bearing a basket of bread and a strong accent that sounded authentic. We placed our orders and he accepted our menus with a flourish.

Sloan reached out as he attempted to retrieve the wine menu. "You mind if we hang on to this?"

"Of course, of course." He hustled away.

I lifted an eyebrow to my companion. "Planning on multiple drinks tonight? I thought we were on the clock. And it's a school night."

Sloan gave me a knowing smile and pulled papers from her purse. She unfolded them between us, leaning in. "I went back over Richard's financial statements, looking for patterns." She scanned her finger down the list of charges. "A lot of his money was withdrawn at ATMs. But a significant number of charges were made in this restaurant." She stopped on a charge listed only as 'Coppola,' made last month for a little over four thousand dollars. "Large charges—as much as ten grand at a time."

"Here?" I thought back over the menu. The fare was not exactly cheap, but definitely not expensive enough to generate that level of tab, even for a roomful of people. "How is that even possible?"

She lifted the wine list. "That's why I wanted to check this. The only thing I can think of is a penchant for expensive wine." Sloan scanned the list and her eyes lit up.

She held the menu toward me and pointed to the final entry. A Bordeaux for nearly four thousand dollars.

My face scrunched at the absurdity. "Don't tell me he comes here to get drunk on bottles of obscenely expensive red wine. Wouldn't a simple Long Island do the trick?"

"Well, the ridiculous wine *could* explain the charges. But I think there's something more going on." She pushed away the menu and nodded her head toward the entrance. A hostess stand stood in what used to be the home's grand two-story foyer.

"You see that staircase by the front door?" She spoke quietly. "Since we got here, several men have come in and headed straight up the stairs. Each alone. Well dressed. I'm curious where the stairs might lead."

"Why, what are you thinking?"

"Did you happen to notice anything about the windows on the way in?"

Definitely not. I glanced to the nearest one. "Like what?"

"Like the downstairs was all lit up like Christmas. But every window on the second floor was completely dark."

I tried to figure out where she was headed. "Which is not likely if people are going in and out."

"Right. Few blinds are that light-proof. There are clearly people up there—and yet to the street it looks empty. A little suspicious, no?"

I pictured Richard being carried out the night before. The place was utterly black, yet somehow he was inside, drunk. It didn't quite make sense at the time, but I hadn't pursued the thought further. I described what I saw to Sloan.

She looked satisfied at the information. "I guarantee whatever's going on up there is what Richard is up to. And I think you should try to find out what it is."

My stomach dropped at her words. I wasn't expecting any real espionage tonight.

"Relax, I said you should *try*," she continued. "I don't think there's any way you'll actually get up there. But if you try, it'll be interesting to see their reaction. Sometimes that's all you need."

I reached for the bread basket to buy myself time. I buttered a crumbly slice and took a bite, considering. What she described sounded reasonable and not very risky. And I had to admit, she was right.

When the hostess stepped away from her perch a moment later, I knocked the crumbs off my hands and stood. Sloan grinned at me in encouragement and grabbed a hunk of bread for herself. I headed straight for the stairs.

I was halfway up when a startled voice sounded behind me. "Excuse me!"

I turned toward the diminutive dark-haired hostess scrambling up the staircase.

"Can I help you?" Her English had only a hint of accent.

I pointed to the second floor. "Isn't there another dining room up here? I wanted to take a peek."

"No." Her face was hard, serious. "That floor is off limits to guests."

"Oh." I gave my best genuinely confused act. "I could've sworn I saw other people going up."

"Private party only." She crossed her arms, looking impatient. "I must ask you to return to your table."

"Of course, I'm sorry. I was on my way to the restroom and this place is just so cute I had to check it out. Where might I find the ladies' room?"

She pointed the direction and I thanked her and scurried down the stairs. The woman held her spot, watching. As I entered the restroom I saw her ascend to speak to a large stone-faced man who appeared at the top of the staircase. Looked like I may have caused a small scene.

I tried to calm my flush before returning to the table. While there was nothing inherently dangerous in what I had been doing, there was still a rush any time I had to lie. It seemed I liked a little deception.

Sloan's grin when I sat down told me she got the same thrill, no matter who was doing the lying.

"We've already had at least three different people poke their heads around the corner, peeking at our table," she whispered. "What exactly did you do?"

I shrugged. "Turns out the upstairs isn't another dining room. They said there's a private party in there. Not allowed up."

She raised her eyebrows at the information. "Interesting."

I took a sip of my wine that had arrived in my absence. A moment later the waiter appeared with our meals. His already-attentive approach seemed possibly kicked up a notch. He definitely wanted us happy. But my creamy alfredo did look delicious.

We devoured our food in silence for a few minutes. Just as I was nearing too full to continue, a figure at the hostess stand made my appetite halt entirely.

I put my fork down and mumbled quietly to Sloan. "The guy up front. Is that who I think it is?"

She caught my vibe and paused before scanning the room nonchalantly. I heard her breath catch before she returned to her meal, a little stiff. "The man from the photos, meeting Richard in the alley. What is he doing here?"

I spared another glance and discovered the man clearly looking in our direction. I quickly averted my eyes. "It can't be a coincidence."

Within seconds the man appeared at the head of our table. He was wearing a fine gray suit with subtle pinstripes not visible from afar. A paisley silk pocket square and slicked-back dark hair gave him a polished, commanding presence. I gulped back my unease.

"Good evening," he began, his accent thick. "I'm Salvatore, the owner of this establishment." He gestured to the table. "I hope everything is to your liking this evening." The smile he directed at us seemed warm on the surface, but his eyes chilled me.

"Everything was excellent." I had to steady my voice. "You have a beautiful place here."

"So wonderful to hear that. Is this your first time visiting?"

We both nodded.

"Lovely, lovely. Well if there is anything you need."

Sloan spoke up. "Actually, we do have a question. We were curious about a wine."

She picked up the menu and pointed to the outrageously-priced bottle at the bottom. "It's unusually expensive, so we figure it must be just amazing. Do you serve it very often?"

"Well," he hedged, "I do have a few select patrons that are fond of the vintage. Very loyal. But I really don't know what they see in it. Overpriced, in my opinion."

"So you don't recommend it?"

"No, no, no. Don't waste your money. Plenty of nice wines on there to choose from that are just as special."

Sloan laid the menu on the table and looked up at him. "Thank you for your advice. We'll steer clear."

The man gave a little bow of his head, his eyes glinting coldly at each of us. "Enjoy the rest of your dinner."

We watched him cross the dining room the way he had come.

I lowered my voice. "Between going upstairs and asking about the wine, I think it's safe to say we're on his watch list."

Sloan nodded. "Probably thinks we're undercover cops or something. I think it's about time to head out of here. We'll pay in cash."

Once we exited, I knew we were both thinking the same thing. We waited until we reached our cars before turning to look back at the facade of the restaurant. The second story was still in shadow, every window pitch black.

Something more going on indeed.

# SEVENTEEN

I tried unsuccessfully to stifle my yawn. A belly full of pasta and wine did not go well with sitting in a dark car for two hours. I sat up straighter, trying to shake myself back into alert mode.

My phone buzzed beside me. I clicked to answer Sloan, who was parked discreetly back near the restaurant to observe any exit by the owner.

"Talk to me," she said. "I'm starting to daydream about my bed."

"I'm with you. This guy better be into something to make this worthwhile."

"I can't guarantee he will be tonight, but I can guarantee he's into something, regardless."

"Why don't you tell me about the wine," I said. "What's your theory—it's a cover?"

"Definitely. What's your best explanation for why the owner would strongly dissuade someone from ordering the most expensive wine on the menu?"

I considered. "Maybe it doesn't exist?"

"Exactly. It's an easy way to launder money. Someone like Richard needs to pass thousands at a time? Just charge up an imaginary bottle of expensive wine. It's especially useful if the guy's running out of cash and has to use credit."

"So what do you think they're covering, exactly?"

"Since it's unlikely they're running a crack den up there, looking at the clientele I'm thinking it's probably gambling. Could be just some poker, but I'd be willing to bet it's a whole sophisticated operation."

I knew nothing of such things. "So you think the restaurant is financially fronting a backroom casino?"

"It certainly wouldn't be the first underground casino, especially in a place like Virginia where most gambling is outlawed. You'd have to head out of state for the nearest legal one."

Fascinating. I had a feeling I'd be amazed at the stuff that goes on behind the scenes around me.

"Hang on." There was a pause. "Okay, get ready. We're finally on the move. Our guy pulled out headed your way. Look for a black Escalade going by."

Instantly I perked up and readied myself to fall in. To avoid showing an obvious tail, Sloan was to stay put near the restaurant for a bit. I could move in behind the owner in question from a parking lot down the road, eliminating any suspicion. This plan only worked if he had headed in the direction we anticipated. Fortunately, we had guessed correctly.

An Escalade zipped by. I pulled out of my spot and eased onto the road, eventually catching up but keeping my distance. I kept Sloan informed of our whereabouts and she headed our way.

The unfamiliar area became more industrial and fairly deserted. I didn't want to stand out. I described the surroundings to Sloan. "I need to hang back a little further."

"I think I know where you're headed." She sounded a little excited. "It's risky, but go ahead and drop way back. I think I know another way there. But I'll really have to hurry."

I let her concentrate while I watched the SUV continue almost out of sight. He was driving exactly the speed limit, never over. Hopefully that would give Sloan extra time to get wherever she was going.

When the Escalade turned again far ahead, deep in a maze of run-down brick industrial buildings, I informed Sloan. She directed me to pull off and wait, then disconnected, leaving me cut off from the action.

I did as instructed and idled, anxiously wondering what was going on. Ten minutes passed. Fifteen. Just when I was about to give in and call Sloan, her name appeared on my phone. I answered hastily.

"He's headed back your way. You might as well just see where he heads, but don't stress about staying on him closely. I'm more interested in this other guy now."

"What other guy?" A dark SUV glided past, headed back the way we had come.

"Explain when I know more." Another disconnect.

Not exactly informative. Less amped this time, I pulled out and got the Escalade back in my sights. Halfway down the road I had a feeling where this was headed. When he pulled back into the parking lot of his restaurant, I felt a little cheated. *All that for a quick errand?*

***

When Sloan notified me she was back in the vicinity, I left my backdoor vigil and met her across the street. Her face glowed with anticipation when I hopped in her car. I perked up again.

"Clearly you saw something. What did you find?"

Sloan grinned and handed me the camera in silence. On the screen was a familiar setting—the alley from the first Richard surveillance, where he had met with the man we now know as the restaurant owner. This time the alley was empty. "I'm confused. Is this from tonight?"

She nodded. "I took it before they arrived. When I heard where he was headed, I had a hunch he would return to the same spot. So I got there first and had a front row seat. Well, front row from a block away."

My eyes widened. "He met with Richard again?"

"Better." She clicked to the next photo. The icy restaurateur appeared, facing a thin, rough-looking younger guy. The scene looked mismatched, Salvatore's fine suit contrasting against the young man's worn, slouchy jeans and hoodie. Thin, bedraggled blond hair grazed his shoulders. Even their postures were opposites, poised stiffness against a youthful casual stance.

Something about the guy's hands stuffed into the hoodie's kangaroo pocket caught my eye. I moved the camera closer, trying to get a better look at the newcomer's outfit.

"Is this what you're looking for?" Sloan clicked again and a close-up of the guy's torso appeared. White Japanese characters glowed from the sleeve of the dark hoodie.

My breath hitched as I registered my recognition. *I know that sweatshirt.* Suddenly the rest of the figure clicked with familiarity. I looked to Sloan. She was clearly waiting for me to catch up.

Before she could speak, a ding chimed from her phone. She checked the screen. "Funeral's over. Richard is headed out."

I stared back, expecting her to explain what I was looking at. The last thing I was concerned about at the moment was Richard's whereabouts. *Who was the guy?*

"We really owe Hannah for all her help." She was maddeningly referring to the text again.

Now I was gaping at her. She gazed back, her face blank.

Finally I gave in. "Well?"

She grinned, amused. "Well, what?"

"It's the same guy from the hotel, right?" My mind was

whirling with the connection. "The last guy to see Carter Evans alive. So who is he?"

"Ohh, that guy," Sloan replied playfully. "I don't know."

Always a game. "Well what did you find out?"

She shrugged. "There, not much. Another exchange, looked pretty similar. Salvatore there always seems to do the receiving. That's definitely a large wad of cash the guy hands him."

"Sounds like he's quite the entrepreneur."

"Exactly. So I did a little checking on him while we were waiting earlier. Apparently he owns those buildings there where they were meeting. An old abandoned factory."

Interesting. "Doesn't sound like a great investment. But I'm guessing it makes a nice quiet spot for his business transactions."

"Exactly. Very out of the way. So we have to wonder who else our guy is doing business with."

She clicked to a new photo. The hoodie reappeared, this time leaning into the passenger window of a rusty silver sedan. The nearby streetlight allowed a glimpse of a rundown residential street behind them.

"He didn't go far. I didn't want to hang around that neighborhood for long, but I got the gist. Our mystery hotel guest is clearly slinging on a street corner. He's a dealer, just as we suspected."

I swallowed, thinking it through. "A dealer with a direct connection to the restaurant owner."

Sloan nodded. "The owner who also met with Richard

in the dark alley. But we don't know for sure what their connection is yet, only that Richard also frequents the restaurant. But that's a few too many coincidences for my taste." She looked at me, her face now serious. "Still think we're chasing an innocent overdose here?"

Well, I *had* wanted all this to lead somewhere for my own entertainment. Unfortunately, so far it only seemed to be leading toward something with our fingerprints all over it. I shook my head gravely in response.

Sloan's eyes darted across the street, the usual lightness returning to her voice. "Well look who just showed up to join the party."

I followed her eyes to the restaurant, where Richard's flashy sports car was pulling into a spot at the front of the parking lot.

"Boy, he sure does like his Italian." She shook her head, her face reflecting the same exhaustion I was beginning to feel. "And I think I've had quite enough of it for tonight."

# EIGHTEEN

I spent most of the next day at work distracted, pondering our next moves in the investigation. I had less than two weeks left before I would have to put my involvement on hold and focus solely on my career. Once I had presented my project and began collecting data for my study, there was no possibility of sneaking off to spy in my free time. I would just be too busy. So we needed to get to the bottom of this as quickly as possible. Unfortunately, I had no experience to tell me what was next.

It seemed Sloan did. After work I headed back to the diner to meet and discuss our plans. And to my surprise, Hannah was at the table with her when I arrived, a round of coffee ready on the table. They both looked up conspiratorially as I settled into my seat.

"So Hannah says she has some inside information for us," Sloan said.

"Oh?" I shook off my jacket. "Anything interesting?"

Hannah looked reluctant. "Maybe. I still feel weird snitching on my boss, but since you said the firm may be in trouble, I thought it could be relevant."

"What did you find?"

Hannah shook her head. "I haven't found anything. I still don't know what I'm looking for. But something a little strange did happen today."

We both gave her our full attention.

"Richard has been coming in looking a little . . . well, rough. Quite a bit lately."

Sloan gave me a quick glance of acknowledgement. "Like, maybe, hungover rough?"

Hannah nodded. "Very possibly. The worse he looks, the crabbier he is. Mainly to me. But today it got so much worse after he had an unscheduled visitor."

I reached for my coffee. "What kind of visitor?"

"I don't know. But it didn't seem like a legitimate business meeting. When the guy showed up and demanded to see him, Richard got all cagey and sent me away on a useless errand. When I got back, the guy was gone and Richard stayed shut up in his office the rest of the day. I had to cancel all his appointments."

"What do you think went on?" Sloan asked.

"I don't know." Hannah looked a little nervous. "But I'm pretty sure they got in a fight or something. He was all disheveled and sweaty, and yelled at me to go away. But when he snuck out at the end of the day, I noticed he had wrapped up his hand in something. I think he might've used his undershirt as a bandage. And I'm pretty sure there was a bruise on his face."

"What did the guy look like?" I asked.

"Brown hair, partially gray. Kind of a big build. Nice suit." Hannah gave a little shiver. "He sort of gave me the creeps. Something about his eyes. Menacing."

I could tell we were thinking the same thing when Sloan turned to me. *Don't tell me it's the same guy.* She reached into her bag and pulled out the camera. After searching the memory to find the photo of Richard meeting the man in the alley, she handed the camera to Hannah.

"Was this the guy?"

Hannah studied the screen for a moment and looked up with widened eyes. "That's him. Who is he?"

Sloan and I exchanged another look. "So far we just know he's the owner of a restaurant Richard frequents," I said. "But we're pretty sure there's a lot more to it than that."

"Actually," Sloan added, "I have confirmation that there is. I checked with a source who confirms there's definitely illegal activity upstairs. Mostly underground gambling. Probably some related enterprises. It's apparently a well-known secret around town."

This was news to me. "Source?"

She winked. "Have to have all sorts of friends in this business." She pointed to the restaurateur on the camera. "He didn't identify himself in any way? Say what it was about?"

Hannah shook her head. "He wouldn't answer any of my questions. Just kept repeating that he needed to see my boss. Immediately. He was almost threatening."

"Okay." Sloan sat back in her seat, lost in thought. "So what do we know about ol' Richie so far?" She counted off on her fingers as she spoke. "He might have a drinking problem. Might be a gambler. Definitely has a lot of debt. And now has some 'menacing' restaurant slash-underground casino owner show up at his workplace, ruffling his feathers. The same restaurant he stumbled out of the other night."

She pointed to the man on the camera screen and continued, her eyes lighting up. "If Richard was a regular at his secret casino, he could've extended him credit. If he has severe money problems—and still goes out gambling and drinking—that could definitely get him into some trouble. He could owe more than just his credit cards."

I picked up on her line of thought. "What if they weren't fighting? Maybe the man was there to rough him up. Give him a little warning."

Sloan slowly nodded. I felt the same excitement at the revelation that I saw in her eyes. We were getting somewhere. We just had to figure out where.

I tried to picture the incident at the office. I pointed to the man in the alley photo. "When he came in to see Richard, would anyone else have heard their conversation?"

Hannah shook her head. "Walter has the only other office

in that section. And he and his new assistant weren't around." She paused, seeming to hesitate. "And that's the other thing. I don't know if it means anything or not."

"Did something else happen?"

"Sort of. No, not really." She looked a little embarrassed. "Never mind."

We both waited patiently, eyebrows raised in interest.

She eventually realized we weren't going to move on. "Okay, fine. Maybe I'm just being silly." She took a deep breath and sighed. "Last week I was replaced. Well, sort of. Officially, I'm Richard's assistant, but for a long time now I've been doing double duty. Handling everything for both brothers. Until last week."

"What happened?" Sloan asked.

Hannah shrugged. "Nothing. That I know of. But the other day a bubbly little blonde waltzes in and announces she's Walter's new assistant."

"Did Walter hire her?" I asked.

She shook her head. "I think it was Richard. He came out and introduced them. Walter seemed just as surprised as I was."

"Well, that seems like it would make your job easier," I said. "But you seem bothered by it."

Hannah's face flushed slightly. "I thought I was doing just fine. I may not understand everything they do, but I do a good job handling their needs. So this just came out of nowhere. I hope I'm not getting fired."

"I'm sure that's not what's happening," Sloan replied.

"Maybe he brought her in for a specific reason. Is she really good at something?"

"Not unless you count primping," Hannah retorted. "They brought in a desk for her, right across from me. Now I look at her all day. She spends most of the day applying lip gloss and fixing her hair. The woman didn't bring framed photos for her desk, she brought a makeup mirror. She looks at that more than the computer screen."

Sloan and I both groaned in sympathy.

"So far, she's been completely useless in learning how to handle things." The frustration in Hannah's voice was growing. "I haven't been able to teach her much of anything. So I'm essentially still doing both jobs. Only she's getting paid, too."

She pulled out her phone and flipped through before handing it over. The screen showed a woman in a low-cut leopard-print top. At first glance she looked young, with bleach-blonde hair and striking features. But upon closer examination, I realized her long eyelashes were fake and her full lips were clearly surgically enhanced. A thick coat of makeup was concealing a face at least a decade older than I first thought, probably two. The woman posed flirtatiously with her hands on her hips, her ample cleavage in plain view.

"I had to get a picture to show you guys," Hannah said. "I told her I needed a photo for a company bulletin board. And this is how she posed for it."

Sloan and I shared another look. This was indeed a little strange.

Sloan turned back to Hannah. "So what does Walter seem to think of her?"

"He's just been coming to me when he needs something, so I have a feeling he has a similar opinion. But he always just goes with the flow. He doesn't like to argue, especially with his brother."

We both studied the picture for another minute.

"You said you're worried about the company," Hannah continued. " I know this tart didn't get the job for her experience. Could she be, like, a spy or something?"

Sloan sighed. "Or something. This does seem fishy, but I'm not sure how yet. Any chance Richard is sleeping with her?"

"Not that I can tell. They really haven't interacted any more since the first day. Around me, anyway."

We were all quiet for a moment, considering. I tried to come up with a plausible explanation for the introduction of this new player into the scenario. If this was Richard's doing, only one possible explanation came to mind. And I had a feeling Sloan was thinking the same thing.

Finally she spoke and confirmed my suspicions. "I think there's a chance Richard *has* planted this woman for some reason. And I can't come up with a noble reason for doing so. Do you think we could come poke around the offices again?"

"To check out this woman?"

"The woman. Richard. Whoever. Like you said, something's not right."

Hannah looked between us, a hint of suspicion taking root. "Wait, I thought you were working *for* Richard. Trying to find a problem in the company. But you keep investigating him instead."

"We are working for Richard," Sloan replied. "And the company could definitely be in trouble. But unfortunately, it's looking like Richard may be a source of some of the problems we're finding."

Hannah did not look mollified. "I don't know. I want to help, but I don't think I should go behind my boss's back any more. This is starting to feel not right."

"I understand," Sloan said, her voice gentle. "You don't have to tell us anything that makes you uncomfortable."

Hannah still looked wary.

Sloan continued. "But please, just keep what we've talked about so far between us. I'm not sure what's going on yet, but I have to follow everything to the end, good or bad. If he fires me first, we can't figure out how to fix things."

Hannah considered her words. She finally nodded in reluctant agreement. "Okay. I certainly don't want to tell him I've been going behind his back, either. But I think I should go."

She gathered her things and slid out of the booth, stopping at the foot of the table. "But Richard and Walter will both be away at the conference for a few days, so I'll have some time alone with the bimbo. I'll see what else I can dig up about her."

Hannah gave us a knowing smile before turning toward the door. Clearly she was not cutting us off completely. And we still had our secret ally.

# NINETEEN

At least my real job was a good excuse not to have to attend the banal-looking conference. Though after a particularly frustrating day with my coworker, I wasn't so sure. While I was busy taking non-stop jabs from Grant, Sloan was handling the long slog through seminars and presentations on up-and-coming investment techniques at a downtown hotel. If there was anything juicy to be uncovered at the event, we figured it would be in the dinner meetings that Richard had demanded be observed.

As I made my way into the hotel after work, I was beginning to question the likelihood of the night's events being worthwhile. I just wasn't much in the mood to waste my evening, and my nerves were fried. I checked in with Sloan via phone. "Okay, let's get this over with."

"Whoa, better restrain that enthusiasm. What crawled up your butt?"

"Sorry, just had a long day. My fellow fourth-year is sort of driving me crazy."

"Rude, or just incompetent?"

"Neither, officially," I replied. "But he has a knack for saying things that seem nice on the surface, but are really just insults if you look closer. I don't know how he does it—but I get it all day long."

"Ah, backhanded compliments. I know them well."

"And the worst part," I said, fuming, "is that if he's saying these things to me, I just know he's slipping them into conversations with my coworkers and supervisors. Subtle sabotage."

"I'd bet you're right. Sounds like he's playing dirty."

"Yeah, I know we're in competition, but seriously. No need for mind games."

"How about if I check this guy out, get a little dirt on him?" Sloan sounded a little too excited by the idea. "Never know when it might come in handy."

Shamefully, I considered it for a brief second. Tempting. "Thanks, but I wouldn't feel right. Besides, this guy is wearing his dirt all over him. His past is basically his own heartwarming tale of redemption he's using to get ahead. They eat it right up."

"Gag. Well, suit yourself. But just say the word."

"Fine. See you in a minute."

I found Sloan at the back of the hotel restaurant but didn't approach, as instructed. Instead I followed her eyes across the bar area, where I spied Walter alone at a table, intently reading. I gave her a subtle nod and moved to a nearby seat to monitor what I had little hope would be anything of interest. So far the guy seemed one of the nicest and most boring I had come across.

After a while of slowly nursing a drink and pretending to be engrossed in my phone, I was bored by the scene and annoyed by my itchy head once again. The wigs were still going to take some getting used to. But I did enjoy the anonymity, and today's chin-length auburn hair was an interesting look for me. I fought the urge to dig my fingernails into my scalp underneath.

Finally I sensed activity nearby and glanced toward Walter. A bottle-blonde hovered above his table, speaking quietly. Her cocktail dress was a little too fitted to her petite figure, and her makeup was a shade on the heavy side. But the overall effect was appealing, I supposed. When Walter hesitated to respond, the woman slid herself into the seat across from him at the table. *Well, this just got interesting.*

I felt pretty confident that his companion was not there to discuss portfolio management. Unfortunately, I couldn't make out what they were saying. The woman smiled coyly, the low cut of her dress emphasizing her cleavage as she leaned toward him. She continued to speak quietly. As usual, Walter didn't return the flirtatious demeanor, but did discard his stack of documents and give her his full attention. His manner and smile were polite, responding but mostly listening.

My phone vibrated with a message from Sloan. She was just as confused by the situation as I was. Unless this guy was a secret billionaire, so far the interactions did not compute. Two different women coming onto him, when he didn't even seem interested? All I could come up was the setting. It seemed plausible that a gathering of financial managers would be a siren call for gold-diggers—which could explain this particular overture, anyway. But for all I knew, money men could live like that all the time.

Before I could respond to the text, Walter's phone lit up with a message as well. He checked it and immediately signaled the waiter for his bill. I quickly readied myself for movement, realizing we hadn't quite discussed a plan for a tail in the hotel, if it came to that. Sloan certainly liked to just wing-it, whether I knew the rules or not.

When Walter made a move to stand, the woman reached to touch his hand. She spoke quietly, her face earnest, almost imploring. Walter smiled gently but removed his hand. With a quick farewell and a nod, he straightened and left. Once he was out the door, Sloan slid off her stool and followed, pulling out her phone.

All that for nothing again? *Why in the world were we here?* My phone buzzed again.

*TALK TO THE WOMAN. WHAT IS HER CONNECTION?*

I glanced back to the attempted seductress. Her face hard with annoyance, she was heading out the opposite exit. I followed causally at a distance.

164

When the woman stopped to pull a pack of cigarettes from her clutch, I caught up and approached cautiously. I had no idea how to handle the situation.

"Excuse me," I said.

She looked up from the open box, a sour look on her face. "No bumming."

I shook my head. "No, sorry to bother you. But that man you were just talking to . . . do you know him?" *Jeez.* Not exactly smooth.

She sighed, her annoyance clear. Her entire demeanor was unrecognizable from the sensual woman in the bar. "Great. What are you, his wife or something?"

I held my hands in the air to show I was harmless. "No, definitely not."

She eyed me suspiciously. "You a cop? You have to tell me."

*Curious.* "No again."

"Then what's it to you? It's a free country."

Clearly I had taken the wrong tack. I was trying to come up with a way forward when I heard the rapid approach of heels and Sloan rounded the corner next to us. She stopped and looked between us, trying to read the situation.

"Hi," she said, feeling us out.

The woman took her in and then glared at the two of us. "Wait. What's going on here?"

Unsure how to proceed, I looked to Sloan.

The woman's eyes narrowed further in our momentary

silence. "You better not tell me they double-booked this guy."

"I don't know," Sloan said carefully. "Looks like they might've. Why would they do that?"

"Like I know," the woman spat back. "The guy's pretty particular. Straight-up shot me down, even though I was playin' his little game just like they said." She looked Sloan over spitefully. "You think you can do any better, go right ahead."

"Maybe they didn't explain the instructions right." I knew Sloan was totally bluffing. "What exactly did they tell you?"

The woman huffed with impatience. "All I know's this guy likes to be picked up. No talk of the business stuff. All been handled already. Wants the 'realistic experience.'"

Sloan shrugged. "Yep, same as they told us."

I hoped I was hiding my reaction to the revelation as well as she was. But inside my mouth was gaping. No way this guy had actually set up something like that. I didn't buy it. And his sending the woman away sealed it. This was a set up.

Sloan continued her feint. "But they said to downplay the look, too. Likes 'em normal."

The woman looked me over once again, this time with amusement. "Clearly. But if that's what he's looking for, he's all yours. Wouldn't be caught dead."

I looked down at my outfit of black pencil skirt and fitted sweater. Looked perfectly respectable to me. I guessed that was the problem.

"Whatever." The woman pulled a smoke from the box and shoved the pack back into her purse. "I've already wasted my night. I'm outta here." She turned on her heel and stalked toward the exit, her fingers fidgeting with the cigarette in her hand.

As we watched her go I quickly shook off the insults, given the source, and turned my thoughts to what we had just learned. Sloan turned to me, her eyes wide and twinkling with the same insight. Clearly we were going to have to adjust our take on the situation.

This changed everything.

# TWENTY

The next night I found myself waiting for Sloan in my newly-acquired hotel room above the conference. I had done a little shopping on the way to quell my nerves. As usual, I had no idea what was supposed to happen next.

My nervous pacing lasted only a few minutes before she burst through the door, arms laden with bags. Her devious smile told me she was looking forward to whatever was coming. And that only made me more apprehensive.

Sloan unzipped a garment bag and pulled out a slinky black dress I recognized from our first outing. It was short and low-cut, but Sloan had pulled it off with class.

She smiled hopefully as she held it up. "What do you think about this?"

"I think you'll look great. So what exactly are you going to be doing?"

Sloan paused as she bit her lip, attempting to hide what looked like amusement. "Sorry to break it to you, but the dress is not for me. It's for you. And your very special role tonight."

I gazed back warily. "What do you mean by 'very special role,' exactly?"

"It means you're the star tonight. I can't be the one to do what needs to be done. Richard could be watching. Keeping tabs on things. If he sees me approach Walter, he'll be on to everything."

"So that's my role—to approach Walter tonight?"

"Yes." Sloan paused, watching me carefully. "As one of Richard's hired escorts."

I gaped at my insane companion. "Excuse me?"

"He already sent one. Probably more than one. That hasn't worked out so far, but we figure he'll try again, right? If he does, you'll take her place. You'll be the one that gives him what he wants."

I didn't like the sound of this. "Which is what, exactly?"

Sloan shrugged. "A photo of him in a compromising position. It's what he asked for."

I shook my head, confused. "I'm not following. So now we're helping set Walter up?"

"Only for show. It's time we filled Walter in on what's been happening. Once we get him alone, maybe together we can finally figure out what's going on. Why we're really here in the first place."

The prospect of answers *was* enticing. I took a moment to wrap my head around my fate. I had never done any real acting, but always wondered if I would have a knack for it. And surely the show wouldn't last very long. I took a deep breath and gave in, consenting for Sloan to have her way with me and my appearance.

An hour later, I admired her handiwork in the mirror. With smoky eyes and glossy lips, the look was a little heavy-handed for my taste but did make me wonder if my usual no-fuss approach was too understated. I could see the appeal. The gentle beachy waves in my hair gave an impression of effortless style I doubted I could ever reproduce. Perhaps a little primping education was in order.

The stretchy material hugging my curves made me uncomfortable, but I had to admit it was quite flattering. I looked at Sloan in the reflection of the mirror. "Have you ever done something like this before? Played a role like this?"

She smiled. "Of course. It's part of the fun."

I could buy that. "So how did you get into a career like this, anyway? Don't tell me a crazy woman began stalking you until you agreed to help."

Sloan gave a quick laugh. But just as quickly her smile faded. She was silent for a moment, eyes not meeting mine. "Actually, that's not as far off as you might think. I got into this because of a boy. Joel. He was a private investigator. Eventually I started helping him with cases, being his sidekick. I fell in love with him. And the job."

"This was the one long-term relationship you mentioned?"

Sloan looked up to face me in the mirror, her face stoic. "My fiancé."

I watched her closely for a moment and waited. The pain I saw creep into her eyes told me she was obviously haunted by something. I didn't want to push.

Finally Sloan spoke again, answering my silent questions. "He was killed on the job early last year. Something went wrong." She looked away. "I wasn't there. And I should've been."

I couldn't even imagine what that must be like. "That's horrible. Did they catch the person responsible?"

Her sigh was heavy. "Never did. I tried piecing it together—I knew some of the case he was working on. But I hit a dead end. Never figured it out."

I waited to see if she would offer more. Sloan stared off into space for a moment. Then she suddenly shook her head, snapping out of her reverie. "Anyway, I had grown a knack for this sort of thing. And I couldn't imagine going back to my former life. I had felt alive doing this with Joel. So I started doing it full time. And here we are."

Sloan reached in front of me to retrieve a sparkling necklace. She gently wrapped it around my neck and secured the clasp. We both admired the stunning piece in the mirror.

"It's your turn," Sloan said. "You can feel the thrill of teasing out the truth. And now you'll look hot doing it."

***

After a long silence, Sloan's voice sounded in my ears. "Okay, I think I've found our buzzard. She's been circling and seems to be going in for the kill."

I looked around the lobby to see if anyone was paying me attention. I knew that as long as I stayed quiet no one would know I was on the phone, but it still seemed strange. Sloan's voice sounded in my ears again.

"And man, he went high-dollar this time. He's not playing around."

I'm sure the bar she was in was nice, but I knew she was not referring to the furnishings. Instead of using our usual short-distance streaming, we were on a normal phone call so I could talk back if I needed. But I could do it without holding the phone to my ear.

"This one is quite striking," she continued. "Long legs, strong bone structure. I'd say retired Eastern European model. Hasn't found the right sugar daddy yet, I suppose."

I tried to hide my smile at her running commentary. As we expected, there appeared to be another escort lined up to bait our target.

"And as usual, he barely registers that she's right beside him. He's more interested in his cheeseburger. I really like this guy."

I waited while she continued keeping an eye on things.

"Oh boy, here comes the flirting. She stole one of his french fries, if you can believe it. Not a bad move. Now he's engaged, anyway."

I stayed ready. We would need to move before anything went too far. It would be much harder to intervene if they left the bar. Although from all we had seen so far, we didn't expect this woman to succeed any more than the others.

"Now a little contact, some flirty touching on the arm. Barf. I better take some quick pictures in case our benefactor checks in and sees this. Hang on."

As I waited for the commentary to return, a voice spoke to me from above.

"Mind if I have a seat?"

I looked up to see a generically-handsome man with salt-and-pepper hair hovering next to me. The well-dressed man fit right in with the moneyed crowd in the lobby. He motioned to the sofa seat next to me.

"Um, no. Go ahead."

He took a seat, casually lounging an arm toward me across the back of the sofa. I gave him a polite smile and pretended to focus on my phone's screen.

The man leaned toward me a little. "You just looked so lonely over here. I had to come say hello."

*Oh, crap.* Maybe I miscalculated by not being clearly on the phone. I wanted to hide it in case Richard happened to see both of us. But it had left me wide open for stragglers.

"Oh, I'm just waiting for someone."

The man kept at it. "Well, is it a boyfriend? Because I can keep you company while you wait."

*This darn outfit she put me in.* "Yes, actually. I'm waiting on my boyfriend."

I heard Sloan's voice return in my ears. "Your boyfriend? What?"

She wouldn't be able to hear anything but my voice. Now Sloan was confused and the man didn't seem deterred by the answer. He grinned and leaned closer.

"Okay. But I'm here and he's not. No harm in getting to know each other in the meantime, right?"

I grimaced internally but gave the man a weak smile. "It's time for me to meet him. I better go."

As I stood to leave, I heard the man grunt his approval. I kept walking, thoroughly disgusted.

Sloan rang in my ears. "Quinn? What's going on?"

I didn't speak up until I was out of view. "Sorry. I think that on me, the outfit definitely gives the impression we were going for. Had to deal with a creep."

"I bet you did, you hot little thing in that dress. But you need to get in here. I think it's time."

\*\*\*

I strode across the lobby into the bar, trying my best not to wobble like an amateur. On impulse this afternoon,

I had purchased a pair of tall black boots with towering heels. They had reminded me of those Sloan was wearing the day we met. In the past I would have never dreamed I could pull them off. I felt like a new person wearing them, as if in disguise. And that seemed fitting for what felt like a whole new life.

I spotted the pair toward the end of the long bar, away from the thin crowd. The suspected high-class escort looked over in annoyance when I climbed onto the stool next to her.

"Hi! How ya'll doin'." I tried out my twangiest southern accent. "Don't cha' just love this place?" I tried in vain to pull the short dress down over my legs.

The woman gave me a tight smile thinly disguising a grimace. His quick nod and smile were more polite. He went back to his french fries.

"So swanky," I announced, pretending to look around the bar in wonder. "Are ya'll here for the conference?"

I heard the woman audibly sigh. She then turned toward me with a face frozen with forced friendliness. She eyed me up and down and seemed about to respond when Walter spoke up.

"I am," he leaned past the woman to respond, his voice friendly. "What about you?"

"Oh, no, not me" I responded, putting my hand to my chest in modesty. "Well, sort of, I guess. I'm here with my boyfriend, Paul. He knows *all* about this stuff. I'm just along for the ride." I shrugged and smiled guilelessly at them.

The woman's fake smile got even bigger as she narrowed her fake eyelashes, glaring at me beyond the view of her prey.

It was time to make a play. "Oh, shoot. I'm so rude. Just jabberin' away over here. My name's Savannah."

I thrust my hand toward Walter, swiping the side of the woman's martini glass in the process. The drink splattered across the woman's dress as it tipped over with a clank. She squealed in shock.

"Oh my goodness." I grabbed for her cocktail napkin. "I'm such a clutz. I'm *so* so sorry." I attempted a pat at her stomach with the napkin.

The woman jumped from her barstool, knocking my hand away. She gaped at me, her face distorted in disgust, then turned and stomped out of the bar.

I had to move quickly. I righted her glass and shifted onto the vacated stool. Walter looked to me in surprise.

I dropped the accent. "Listen, we only have a few minutes."

Walter's eyes widened. "Excuse me?"

I lowered my voice. "That woman was paid to seduce you. You're being set up."

His face froze as he absorbed my words. I sensed his body tense.

I smiled cheerfully and leaned into him. "But someone could be watching. So you need to pretend like nothing's wrong. Smile at me."

His face looked panicked momentarily. He stared at the

bar top, pondering. Then he took a deep breath and looked back at me questioningly, with a wary smile.

I tilted my head, my voice gentle. "Has anything seemed a little odd lately?" I looked at him earnestly. "Have you noticed an unusual number of women approaching you, being forward with you?"

He stared back at me momentarily and then looked away. I could see the recognition churning in his mind as his eyes darted aimlessly.

I placed my hand gently on his forearm and gave him a confident grin. "I'm here to help you get out of it." I kept my voice quiet. "I know you have no reason to, but you're going to have to trust me."

He raked his hand slowly across the lower part of his face, letting out a long breath. When he reached for his drink, his hand was shaking slightly. I let him sip quietly in thought for a moment.

He looked up at me and nodded imperceptibly. I stood and leaned in close, placing my hand on his back. "She's going to be back any minute," I whispered into his ear. "I need you to come with me. I'll explain everything."

# TWENTY-ONE

I swiped the keycard and entered my hotel room. Walter looked both ways down the corridor before hesitantly following me in.

"Make yourself comfortable," I said, tossing my key onto the table. I headed straight to the door to the adjoining room, flipped the lock and opened the door.

"Okay," I called out.

I heard a lock click on the other side, and the complementary door quickly opened. Sloan strode into the room in jeans and a tank top, looking serious.

Walter backed toward the front door, anxious. "What is this?"

"You should probably sit down," Sloan said matter-of-factly.

I gave Walter a reassuring look. "This is Sloan. She's a private investigator hired by your brother. Richard."

"Dicky?" he said. "Why would he hire an investigator?"

"That's what we want to talk to you about." Taking a

seat at the head of one of the double beds, I motioned for him to do the same on the opposite. He complied.

"As you might have guessed," I began calmly, "my name's not really Savannah. I'm Quinn. I've sort of been helping with the investigation."

He loosened his tie nervously. "What investigation?"

I motioned toward Sloan, still standing near the doorway with her arms crossed. "Your brother hired Sloan to get pictures of you in a compromising position. He wanted proof that you are having an affair." I looked him in the eye. "Before we go any further, tell us the truth. Are you involved in an affair?"

"No," Walter replied, aghast. "Absolutely not. He knows that."

"That's what we thought. We believe you."

He shook his head, bewildered. "He hired you to take pictures of me? Why would he think I was cheating?"

I glanced at Sloan. She was holding back, waiting for my lead. I nodded for her to jump in.

"We don't think he actually believed anything he told me," she said, moving closer.

Walter turned to her, quizzical.

"We think your brother was trying to set you up. We believe he wanted photographs of you in a compromising position, real or faked, so that he could use them for something. We were hoping you could shed some light on what that something is."

He looked at me in confusion. "So that woman—those

women—they were a setup?" He looked dazed. "By my own brother?"

I nodded my head solemnly and gave him a sympathetic smile.

"Why would your brother want photos like that? Do you think he would want to blackmail you?"

"No." Walter shook his head. "There has to be another explanation."

I probed again. "Can you think of anything he could do with suggestive pictures of you?"

Walter looked toward the floor, lost in thought.

I continued. "What about this special deal being worked out with Quandom? We know he's pushing for the deal, but you're against it. And he lied to us about that. Could that have anything to do with it?"

Walter suddenly drew a sharp breath. He looked between Sloan and I, his eyes wild with realization. He jumped to his feet and crossed the room. I was afraid he was going to walk out. Instead we watched in silence as he paced the floor, running his hands through his thinning hair.

Finally he stopped and looked up at Sloan. "So let me get this straight: my brother paid you to get pictures of me with a woman.'"

"He did."

"And you suspect he also paid women to get me in these photos."

"We know for sure that someone did," I said. "What would pictures like this do for your brother?"

Walter looked at us soberly. "I know exactly what he could do with those photos."

He moved back to the bed and sank heavily. "The question is why."

Sloan moved near. "His claim was that he was trying to protect the business. He told me it was a family company that could have its reputation ruined if you were unfaithful."

Walter nodded. "That's exactly right, that's what we thought." He looked up at us. "Which is why we set up a rule in the by-laws that kicked anyone on the board of directors out of power if they did anything that could embarrass the company. 'Conduct unbecoming of a member,' it's called."

I began to understand. "So if he had evidence implicating you in a scandal, you would lose your power in your own company."

He nodded. "The board would have no choice but to vote me out."

"But why now?" Sloan asked. "Why would he want to get rid of you?"

Walter stared at his knotted hands. "With me gone, Richard would have the majority he needs to push the deal with Quandom Corporation through. I made it clear I'm not giving in on it."

I stood up to think. "So he sets you up, and gets the business deal he wants. It must be pretty important for him to sell out his own brother." I looked back at Walter.

"We think we know about the technology and how lucrative having a time advantage would be. So then what is your objection?"

"I was all for it in the beginning." Walter bent and rubbed his temples, his face pained. "My problem is with the terms Quandom is asking for. In exchange for exclusive use of their technology for a set time—enough to potentially make a fortune—they want a large share in our firm. A stake equal to mine or my brother's. Everyone's share would be reduced in order to offer it."

Sloan jumped in. "So then would that give them extra power in the company?"

"No more than anyone else, with that alone. But I don't like the vulnerability inherent in a deal like that. It makes us ripe for a takeover."

"A takeover," I mused aloud. "Even in a privately-held company? How would something like that work?"

"With my brother and I as co-owners, holding the biggest shares by a large margin, there's little threat from outsiders," he explained patiently. "But this introduction of a new slice of the pie changes all that."

He stood and began moving again, looking restless. "Once they have that large of a stake, if they were able to convince a couple other major shareholders to sell their stakes, they would be able to take control of the company."

"And you don't want to take the risk, so he had to find a way around you in order to get a deal," Sloan said.

Walter looked dismayed. "So it seems."

"Well, if it makes you feel any better, it looks like there may be a reason your brother would go to such lengths to make the deal go through. Besides pure greed."

Walter stopped and looked at Sloan, curious.

"We think he's in trouble, and not just from the credit card companies. He owes a lot of money, most likely from gambling. Did you know Richard is deep in debt?"

He shook his head. "I knew Richard liked to play now and then, but no, I had no idea there was a real problem."

He looked grave as he was lost in thought again. Suddenly his face darkened. "Oh. No, I think I understand now." He shook his head as though in disbelief. "I never even considered the threat of takeover would come from my own brother. They wouldn't even need another shareholder."

I was confused. "What do you mean?"

"I know what's happening. If this deal goes through, sure, it could mean a lot of money. A whole lot. But we would have to proceed slowly in order to avoid immediate attention. Small trades at a time. It would take time. Certainly wouldn't fix gambling debts overnight." He started pacing again, speaking more quickly. "But if he pushed the deal through, giving a large share of our firm to Quandom—and then he secretly sold his own shares over to them as well—he could net enough from the sale to pay off any debts, and still retire semi-comfortably. Or heck, he might even have an agreement to keep his job.

While the rest of us would lose all control of our firm. It would no longer be the family business, and we could all be fired."

He stopped moving and looked at us in bewilderment. "He must've been planning this with Carolyn Evans from the beginning. Finding an escape route by selling us all out."

We were all silent for a moment, considering his theory.

Finally Sloan spoke again. "So with everything he already had to do for this deal, I'm guessing he would've gone to great lengths to protect it. What do you know about Carolyn's husband? Would he have played a role in this?"

"Actually, this deal was first conceived when he was still in charge of his company. Richard tried to make a deal, and Carter refused. The current version of the deal that includes the ownership stake was only offered after Carter was sent to rehab. Carolyn took over in his absence and made the new proposal."

Sloan and I exchanged a look, clearly thinking along the same path.

Walter tried to read our silent conversation. "Why, you think Carter was in on this?"

"Just the opposite." I looked him in the eye. "It looks like he may have tried to get in the way."

My meaning sunk in and Walter gaped at us. "Please tell me you aren't thinking that Richard had something to do with Carter's death. It was an accident."

Sloan moved closer. "Well, now that we know all this, doesn't it seem convenient that the soon-to-be-ex-husband—who wanted to jeopardize the deal—shows back up, and almost immediately ends up dead?"

Walter didn't look convinced. "A sad coincidence. He was an addict."

"As far as we can tell, he was trying to slip back into his old life. Make up with his wife. It's safe to assume he wanted control of the company back as well, which would've spoiled everything at the last minute."

"No way," Walter insisted. "My brother might've made a desperate move to make money, but I refuse to believe he could've hurt anyone. Much less killed them."

"We don't think he did anything directly," I interjected. "But there is something you should see."

Sloan moved to the desk and pulled three photographs from a drawer. She flipped the switch to illuminate the desk lamp and laid the first photo out for Walter to see. He hesitated distrustfully before leaning in to examine. It was the same photo she had originally used to drag me further into all of this.

"This is your brother having a discussion in a dark alley. Money was exchanged." She pointed to Salvatore in the photo. "This guy owns the Italian restaurant your brother likes to visit. You know the one? I believe you've had to drag him home on occasion."

Walter regarded her quizzically, probably wondering how Sloan knew such a detail. She offered no explanation.

"He's not just there for the wine," I added. "The upstairs is an illegal gambling operation. Runs nightly as far as we can tell. Richard is quite the regular."

Walter's eyes widened. "I had no idea."

I continued, pointing to Salvatore. "This creepy man also reportedly came by the office and roughed Richard up a little recently. Pretty sure your brother's in deep to this guy, and based on the frequency of his visits to the restaurant, getting deeper every day."

Sloan added the second photograph, showing Salvatore in the alley with the young mystery dealer. "Here's the entrepreneur again in his favorite secret meeting spot, this time with one of his 'business associates.' Not surprisingly, this guy is definitely a drug dealer. And not a terribly discreet one at that. I found him slinging on a street corner not too far away."

She laid the final photo on the desktop. "And finally, this is the same young dealer leaving a private party with our former CEO. Very private. Just the two of them in the hotel room." She looked somberly at Walter. "On the night he overdosed."

Walter met her gaze and stepped back in horror. We let him process silently for a moment.

Sloan continued softly. "Now, it is possible that Carter simply fell back into old habits and went too far. Of course that's a possibility. But there is a direct link back to your brother, with secret money changing hands. And a reason to want him out of the picture."

I tried to assist. "And by trying to set you up, Richard has definitely shown he'll cross some lines. So we have to at least consider that it's not all a coincidence. That it's all means to the same end."

Walter sank to the bed behind him. He leaned forward, elbows on his knees, and scratched his hands through his hair. We left him to work through things for a few minutes.

Finally he spoke, his resolve returned. "No. I believe my brother may have made some terrible, selfish choices when he felt backed into a corner. But I still refuse to believe he had anything to do with murder."

"Fair enough," Sloan said. "But there's still the issue of him clearly setting you up."

I moved closer. "We need to stop his plan to ruin you, and find out the truth. And we may have a way to do both."

He regarded us carefully. "How?"

"Well, he wants pictures of you in a compromising position." Sloan's face broke into a mischievous grin. "We start by giving him some."

# TWENTY-TWO

Two days later I found myself back in the parking lot of Westbrook Trading with Sloan. Rather than watching for a target to tail, this time we were waiting on him to leave. I had a suspicion I was itching to check out.

"I'm feeling weird about all the vague not–quite–lies we've been telling Hannah," I said. "Now that we're zeroing in on Richard, can we fill her in on what's going on?"

Sloan nodded. "I'm thinking the same thing. It's time she learns what her boss may really be up to."

A moment later we saw Richard trudge through the front doors and squeeze himself into his sports car. Soon after we got a glimpse of the new assistant. She tottered across the lot on stiletto heels, her hairspray–stiff blonde hair blowing awkwardly in the wind. Her tight skirt was so short she had to continuously pull on it as she walked to keep from becoming truly indecent. At least she had *some* shame, I supposed.

As soon as she exited the lot, we headed for the building. When we turned the corner to the executive suite we found Hannah, alone at her desk. She hopped up anxiously.

"I sent the other assistant home, like you asked. What's going on?"

"Walter will be here soon," Sloan replied. "We'll explain everything when he gets here. In the meantime we need to take a look around his office. Richard is gone for the day, right?"

"All done."

"Good." Sloan pulled two handheld electronic devices from her bag and looked to me, eyebrows raised. "Let's check out your theory, then."

Looking confused but playing along, Hannah reached to open Walter's office door. Sloan stopped her.

"Hang on," she said. She flipped two switches on the first device in her hand, lighting green LED lights on the front. Satisfied, she left it on the desk beside her. "Okay, we're clear."

We entered Walter's office. It was basically a mirror-image of Richard's. Same landscaped view out the large windows. But Sloan was interested in the identical furnishings and fixtures contained within. She began slowly waving the second device across every available surface in the room, beginning with the walls.

Hannah watched from the doorway, clearly unsure what to make of the situation. When Sloan stepped onto a chair to reach an overhead light, Hannah finally spoke up. "So what's going on, exactly?"

The device stayed silent, clearing the light fixture. Sloan stepped down and moved toward the desk. Before we could fill her in, a loud beep sounded from her hand as she swept across the surface.

"Oh boy," Sloan said. "What do we have here?"

She narrowed the offending signal to a small metal dragon figurine sitting on Walter's desktop. Sloan picked it up and examined the item. She then held it out to us, pointing to a small round indentation in the corner.

I couldn't believe I was right. "Is that what I think it is?"

"Looks like it." Sloan turned to Hannah. "Where did this come from? Did his new assistant give it to him?"

"No." Hannah hesitated, looking uncomfortable. "I did."

We both stared at her, waiting for explanation.

"Well, sort of," she continued. "It was a gift. Blaine wanted me to give it to him."

*Richard's son.* Of course. Sloan and I looked at each other.

Hannah watched us warily. "What?"

Sloan continued her interrogation. "Did you put it on here on his desk? So it's looking right at him?"

Hannah shrugged. "He told me to. Said it was sentimental or something." Her voice became more emphatic. "What's going on?"

I couldn't keep her hanging any longer. "You seem to have inadvertently planted a hidden camera in Walter's office."

Her eyes grew round. "From Blaine? "

"From Richard, most likely," I replied. "Blaine was just the means, like you. He may or may not have known what it was. Not sure yet."

"What? Why would Richard do such a thing?"

Sloan spoke up. "To monitor his interactions with his new assistant, is our best guess. Did this show up here about the same time she did?"

Hannah nodded, looking dumbfounded.

"Well, by what you've told us, I doubt he got anything useful." Sloan turned to me, her annoyance clear. "Looks like he was hedging his bets. Trying to make sure there were opportunities inside the office, too. In case I didn't catch anything."

"Catch anything . . . like what?" Hannah was getting nervous. "Is Walter a criminal?"

"Not Walter," I said. "But his brother is making a pretty good case for himself."

Hannah shook her head in confusion. "Richard? I don't understand. Why would Richard trick me into planting a camera in here?"

Time to let her in.

"He's trying to get photos of Walter in a compromising position," Sloan answered. "That's why he hired me, under the ruse of protecting the company from scandal."

"Wouldn't have it any other way," Sloan said. "I don't appreciate being used to set up innocent people."

"I just hope we finally get to the truth," I added. "This was a lot more than I bargained for."

We heard a ding. Walter retrieved his phone from his pocket and checked the screen.

"My brother just called for an emergency board meeting for day after tomorrow," he said. "And he wants to meet with me in advance. Looks like he's not going to waste any time trying to get rid of me."

Sloan smiled confidently. "Guess we'll have to move our private little meeting with him up to tomorrow, then. We'll be looking forward to it."

# TWENTY-THREE

I couldn't decide if anxious or exhilarated was a better descriptor. I paced the floor of Walter's office in silence, wishing things would just get going already. What in the world was I doing here?

But everything so far had led up to this. We were finally going to get some answers.

I rechecked the office door for the tenth time, making extra sure it was locked. The last thing we needed was to spoil the surprise with an unannounced entry. As long as we stayed in silent mode, Richard would have no reason to try to come in. He was busy getting ready for what he thought was a masterful coup. And he would be oh-so wrong.

Sloan peeked her eyes open at me from her position on the floor. She smirked at my obvious nervousness and closed her eyes, returning to her Zen-like state. Now, I'm no stranger to yoga and meditation, but I was awed at her ability to be so calm and collected at a time like that. I was far from discovering inner peace. Maybe that was actually the secret to her cool.

A low beep sounded from the speakerphone on the desk, followed by Hannah's whispered voice. "Here we go, guys."

Sloan sprang up, following me to the chairs we had gathered in front of the phone. The input changed and we heard male voices. Walter had just entered Richard's office and they were concluding their greetings. A little chit chat about golf, with Walter playing along nicely. I was impressed at his ability to fake geniality with his backstabbing brother. I would be tempted to strangle him.

With pleasantries taken care of, Richard teed up. "So listen, Walter, we have a little situation here."

"I'm all ears."

"It's come to my attention that there has been some, shall we say, unseemly conduct on your part."

Walter hesitated. "What are you talking about?"

"I'm talking about your 'extracurricular activities.' At the conference." Richard paused, letting his words hang a moment. "Now, I take partial responsibility here, because I did send you to that hotel and I cancelled our dinner meeting, leaving you there by yourself. But you're going to have to take responsibility for your own actions, too."

"I really don't know what you're talking about, Richard."

"The woman at the bar. The one you followed to her room. I know."

Walter didn't respond right away. When he did his tone had altered. "What could you possibly know about it? And just how would you know about her?"

"Let's just say it was brought to my attention. The specifics are not important. What *is* important is what we're going to do about it."

"I'd say the specifics are pretty damn important." He injected just the right amount of outrage into his voice. "What business is it of yours?"

"Look, I'm not judging." Richard tried to sound conciliatory. "I agree, your marriage is your business. But the fact that someone could get this information, to bring it to my attention, is the whole point. Anyone could have access to it."

"I can't believe this. What if I told you nothing happened?"

"I'd believe you, of course. You're my brother. But unfortunately, these things are out of my hands. You know how it is."

"What is that supposed that mean?"

"It means we set up rules to protect the image of the firm, Wallie. So it doesn't matter what the truth is. You could've gone in there to give her tutoring on the stock market for all I know. But you broke the rules. It looks bad. It leaves room for all sorts of speculation we don't need, especially now. We'll have to take action before this damage spreads."

"What sort of action?" Walter's voice increased, beginning to sound frantic. "Is that what this emergency meeting is about? Just what are you up to, Richard?"

"Only doing the best for the firm," Richard replied calmly. "You'd do the same in my shoes."

"So you're, what, calling a vote? Going to force me out? Based on what? You have no proof."

"I'm sorry to say you're wrong, little brother."

We heard the sound of a drawer scraping open and shut. I knew he was proudly presenting the staged photos of me and Walter looking chummy as he left the hotel room. We had left little room for interpretation. There was a pause for Walter's silent reaction.

"Regardless of what happened," Richard continued, "we both know this doesn't look like tutoring. And if I have these, so could someone else. We can't take any chances. I'm obligated to turn this over."

"So that's it then." Walter sounded flat, as though resigning himself to his unemployed fate. But I knew it was really a sad acknowledgment of the end of their relationship. He gave him one last chance. "You've decided, and I'm out."

"I'm sorry, Walter." Richard's slimy voice actually had the nerve to sound genuine. It made me sick.

I began to tense. It was nearing time for us to jump in. The men sat in silence for a full minute, tension crackling between them for very different reasons. I almost felt bad for what was about to happen.

Finally Walter broke the silence, his voice now acidic. "Well, there's just one catch here, *big brother.*"

Sloan raised her eyebrows at me in question, and I replied with a nod. She reached to unlock the office door.

"Oh yeah?" Richard sounded like he was humoring him. "And what's that?"

Silently we crossed the hall, past Hannah intently listening in from her desk. She gave us a nervous thumbs up as we reached Richard's office. Sloan flung the door open with a flourish, crashing the handle against the wall. The girl knows how to make an entrance.

Richard startled at the sound. Walter didn't turn around, didn't even flinch. He kept his eyes trained on his brother. He was going to enjoy this.

Richard was instantly alarmed at the sight of Sloan in the doorway. "What are you doing here?"

Sloan stalked into the room, a smug grin on her face. "There's just one little thing I left out, boss. Thought you might want to know."

That was my cue. I waltzed into the room and straight toward Richard. He eyed me with confusion for a moment before his eyes widened with recognition. He snatched the photos from the desk and the confirmation played out on his face. I was dressed identically to the night in the photos, so there would be no mistaking. He glared at both of us with suspicion.

Sloan gestured toward me. "I think I forgot to introduce you to my good friend. Quinn. Of course, you've seen her before. She does do a little modeling. But I think it's time you two finally met."

I gave a little wave, barely suppressing my grin.

Richard slammed the photos on the desk and jumped to his feet. "What the hell is going on here?"

Sloan and I turned to Walter, looking relaxed in his chair. He sat forward and cleared his throat, taking his time before speaking.

"Richard, you should know that those photos of yours are faked. Unlike you, I've never cheated, or anything close. And you know that. But that didn't stop you from trying every way you could to fabricate evidence that I have."

Richard's mouth gaped as he fumbled to find a response.

Walter waved his hand. "Save it. I obviously know about the investigator here. And we all know about the other women you tried to involve in your little scheme. Your plan to hand over our firm, leaving the rest of us hung out to dry. We know everything."

His brother only stared, the color fleeing his face as quickly as it had come.

Walter continued. "So all I have to say to you right now is . . . why?"

Richard visibly fought acceptance of the situation. He glared between all of us, his breath heavy. The awkward moment must have felt like an eternity to the floundering fraud. Finally he seemed to grasp his reality and sank back to his chair, looking dazed.

Walter continued. "Your gambling problem? Is that why you would sell your own brother out—to get yourself out of debt?"

Richard shook his head, coming back to life. He looked at his brother earnestly. "I would've found a way to get you back in. I . . . I was desperate. They were going to take everything. I would've jeopardized the firm anyway. This way I could stay involved, I was assured I would have a place at the new firm. And I wanted to try to bring you on, after everything settled down."

"So let me get this straight," Walter said, taking his time. "You admit that you did in fact set me up. Tried to get evidence of *unseemly conduct*, as you put it, by any means necessary, in order to get me kicked off the board. All so you could sell out and let Carolyn Evans take over the firm. And it sounds like you would walk away with a job and your debt paid off, while we're out in the cold. Do I have that all correct?"

Richard was seeming very nervous by now. "But like I said, I was going to try to take care of you. You have to believe me."

Walter stared at his brother with a coldness I would never have thought possible from such an amiable man. "Brother, I'm never going to believe anything you say again."

Richard returned the gaze, disbelief morphing into an understanding of his situation. His eyes settled on the desktop, wheels turning. When he looked up again, his expression had turned hopeful.

"But luckily it's not too late," he stammered. "I'll . . . I'll cancel the meeting right now. Just forget everything. I was stupid and selfish and I know you hate me. Rightfully so. But I'll make it up to you. I'll do anything. I'll even get help for my problem if you want. I know I have a problem." Richard looked almost repentant. "And maybe in time, you'll forgive me."

"Actually, there's no need to cancel the meeting." Walter's icy demeanor did not falter. "What if I told you you just admitted everything to the entire board? That they just heard every word—every sordid little detail?"

The remaining color drained from Richard's red face. He gaped in horror at his brother. "You set *me* up? How could you—I could lose everything! How could you do this?"

Walter's only response was a continued calm repose. Richard stared for another moment, grasping his fate, before he decided to flee. He had his hand on the doorknob when his brother finally spoke again.

"Actually, now I'm the liar," Walter said to the room, his back to Richard.

Richard paused, considering the words. He looked back at his brother.

"Well, I only proposed a hypothetical. So not *technically* a lie. But you should know the board was not listening. They don't know anything. *Yet.*"

Relief instantly washed over Richard, turning quickly to confusion. Timid, he returned to his side of the desk, approaching Walter as though nearing a wild animal.

"See, there's just one more thing we haven't cleared up yet," Walter continued. "Carolyn's husband, Carter. How does he play into all this?"

Richard scoffed. "He doesn't. Absolutely nothing to do with any of it."

Walter raised his voice for the first time. "Enough!"

Richard shrank back, clearly surprised to see his normally docile brother so heated.

Walter regained his composure. "Here's the situation. We hold your future in our hands right now. I could've had the board listening in on all of this. Ruined you on the spot. There's probably a few laws you've broken in there as well. But I want to give you one last chance to fess up. Did you or did you not have anything to do with Carter Evans' death?"

"No," Richard replied, emphatic.

"Ok. But you should know that we have evidence suggesting otherwise. Payoffs clearly linking you to the young drug dealer who was the last to see Carter alive."

Richard stiffened.

"But there are a few links in that chain. So maybe you weren't responsible—but you know something about it?"

Clearly uncomfortable but resolute, Richard gazed back without a word.

"I'm really going to need more, Richard. Or we'll be forced to share everything we know with the authorities. Let them sort it out."

Finally grasping the situation, Richard's eyes went wide and began darting around the room wildly. I was afraid he might've stopped breathing. Finally his panic seemed to settle as he appeared to come to a decision. He took a deep breath and looked his brother in the eye, solemn.

"I swear I didn't set up Carter's death. I swear on my son's life. But I'm pretty sure I know who did."

# TWENTY-FOUR

I knew I was supposed to play it cool, to look like we've been expecting such confessions all along. But I was stunned. Some truly underhanded things really had gone on, many things, and we'd successfully uncovered them. And the ugliness was only going deeper.

Richard held up his hands in a 'hold-up' gesture. "What I mean is—*if* someone had anything to do with his death, then I may know who. But I don't know for sure that anyone did. I don't want to know."

"Okay. We're listening. Tell us what you *do* know."

Richard glared back, his vulnerability seeming to dissipate. He stood from his chair, towering over his brother. "And if I do, my 'indiscretions' will be kept under wraps?"

"I'll tell you what." Walter did not appear intimidated by his brother's renewed confidence. "You tell us everything you know. Everything. And I'll keep your attempts to ruin me and the firm to myself. Any other

207

crimes you may admit to, well, I'll have to decide as we go. But you'll step down from the board. Effective immediately."

Richard took a deep breath, his glare intensifying. But he didn't try to argue.

"And if we find out you've lied about any of this, everything is fair game. It's all coming out."

Richard shut his eyes for a moment, processing his situation. When he reopened them, he looked defeated. The fight had gone out of his eyes. "My actions may have helped lead to his death. I'm not certain. But it certainly wasn't on purpose."

Richard sat heavily back in his chair. "It was my idea, in part. Carter showed back up and was threatening to shut us down, shut the entire deal down. We were so close. So I simply suggested Carolyn could 'accidentally' derail his sobriety. It would've happened anyway. Just help him along a little. If he used again, there'd be no way he could make decisions for his company again. We could do what we needed to do."

Walter's voice was quiet, concerned. "So you planned for him to overdose?"

"Of course not. She was just supposed to get some of his favorite stuff, and leave it where he could find it. She was convinced he would give in and start using again. Then she could have the company call for a drug test and bust him. At the very least, she could plant it on him. If the firm even thought he was using, it could buy us enough time."

Walter's prodding was gentle. "So what happened?"

Richard shook his head. "That's all I know. All I did was make the connection. I don't touch the stuff, but I know people . . . that know people." He shrugged. "I put her in touch. Whatever she did from there, I have no idea. I swear."

I had to know. "So your 'people.' Would that include Salvatore? Who you owe a lot of money to?"

He smirked. "You guys really did do your homework. Yeah, he's my guy. I happen to know he's a well-rounded businessman, has his hands in a lot of pots. So I sent him a referral. That's it."

Walter leaned forward, considering. "So when Carter turned up dead, didn't you wonder what went wrong? Did you ever ask her what happened?"

"None of my business. Asking questions like that, well, no good can come from it. I know a little about getting mixed up with the wrong people. You keep your head down and eyes forward. Let 'em do whatever they're gonna do." Richard glanced at each of us, looking sincere. "But whatever our differences, I liked the guy. I wouldn't have wanted to do him any real harm. I'm not a monster."

I didn't know why, but I actually believed him this time. I was pretty sure Richard didn't do anything to Carter. But where did that leave us?

"So what I'm hearing," Sloan mused out loud, "is that you played matchmaker for a drug deal that turned into an overdose. An overdose that may have been accidental—

209

but given the motivations here, it could've been intentional. So how do we figure out which?"

Richard scoffed. "What are you going to do, go ask them nicely? If I were you, I'd just let it go. What's done is done."

"Sorry, I don't work that way." Sloan's smile was cold.

I jumped in the mix. "Maybe we should just take what we know to the police. Surely we can keep Richard's name out of it?"

"That's not our agreement," Richard fumed.

Sloan held up a hand to calm him. "Don't worry, that's not the play. The problem is she would just lawyer up immediately. A woman with means like that—they'd never get anywhere. Our only chance is before she has any idea anyone is on to her."

She paused for a moment, considering, before her face lit up. "Although there *is* someone who could be on to her." She turned to Walter. "I have an idea for how to get the story out of Carolyn, so we can finally settle this once and for all. But we're going to need the support of everyone in this room." She raised an eyebrow but avoided looking in Richard's direction.

Walter got the hint. "Oh, Richard. We're going to need your help."

"Forget it," he retorted. "I kept my end of the bargain, I told you what I know. That's *everything*. And I'm off the hook."

"You're right, you are off the hook. With the *firm*. But

what about all that money you owe your friend Salvatore—are you off the hook on that? How are you going to keep him happy without a job?"

The smugness melted from Richard's face, replaced by another dazed expression. It appeared he hadn't thought that far ahead yet. And I bet the road looked awfully bleak. After a moment he met his brother's gaze again, contrite. "So what are you proposing?"

Walter glanced at both of us, considering. I was curious myself. He took a deep breath and turned back to Richard.

"Well, unlike you, I actually care if your life is ruined."

Richard's eyes immediately lowered. He looked vaguely ill.

"But I really want to get this whole thing settled. To do that, we're going to need the rest of the story. So, you assist these ladies with whatever they need to get that story. And I'll bail you out."

Richard's eyes peeked back up at his brother.

Walter appeared to be coming up with a plan as he spoke. "Not only will I keep your secret plan from the board, but I'll pay off your gambling debt. The last thing we need threatening the firm is some criminal enterprise. Then myself and the rest of the board will quietly buy out your stake. You can use that to have a nice, peaceful early retirement. Assuming you get your problem under wraps, you should be quite comfortable. But I won't bail you out again."

Richard looked a mixture of relieved and suspicious. "But after all that, why would you do that for me?"

Walter sighed. "Because you're still my brother. And I'm not going to let you be threatened by gangsters. But I'm afraid we won't have much of a relationship going forward. This will likely be it for us."

I felt the weight of the loss between them as they sat in silence. I couldn't imagine that level of betrayal—or guilt. Their locked eyes held opposing strains of pain. Finally Richard's broke away just as welling tears threatened to escape. He blinked them back and looked up at me and Sloan, his face drooping with resignation.

"What do you need me to do?"

# TWENTY-FIVE

Useful vandalism, she'd called it. I just hoped someone else wouldn't call it a *felony*. I pushed the hood of my sweatshirt down away from my face, glad to have the task over with. We had made our escape seemingly unnoticed, and I felt my shoulders relax a little more the further we got from the parking lot of Quandom. I had to admit, that too was a little fun.

I turned to Sloan at the wheel. She looked calm and content, as usual, a small smile hinting at her mutual enjoyment.

"So you really think that's sufficient to put the scare into Carolyn Evans?"

She shrugged. "I'd be pretty freaked, wouldn't you?"

I considered and nodded with agreement. We had done quite a number on her car. Nothing permanent, of course. Just a little fake blood and creepy drawings of headstones on her Mercedes as it sat in the mostly empty lot. I'm not much of an artist. But all perfectly washable. No harm done—except psychologically. We hoped, anyway.

Sloan had taken care of the preliminary assaults. First, an anonymous letter suggesting someone knew what she had done—leaving the details vague to allow room for interpretation. With a hint that a future ransom would suffice for shutting them up. Followed by several eerie phone calls from a burner involving nothing but heavy breathing. I got a little weirded out just thinking about it, and I got to be one of the heavy breathers. I did feel pretty confident we had laid enough groundwork. The car should push Carolyn over the edge.

"I trust you not to get me arrested, you know," I said. "I'm not sure my work would appreciate vandalism on my record."

"I know, I know. Speaking of your job, is Grant still bothering you?"

I shrugged. "I definitely dread him every day, but I'm kind of getting used to it. It's just his way, I guess. He did have a difficult time for a while there. Why?"

"Well . . . about that. So his big backstory is that he was arrested as a teenager, dropped out of high school and ended up homeless for a while, right?"

I nodded. "He's implied he had to do questionable things during that time, but I haven't asked for any more details. But supposedly he pulled himself together, got his GED, and did some college online before going full-time normal college student and making it to a top graduate school. I guess that *is* pretty remarkable."

A thought occurred to me. "But hold on. I don't remember telling you about his backstory, only that he uses it."

"Yeah, that's true. It was on his internship application. He wrote a lovely essay about it."

*Oh, no.* What had she been up to? "And exactly how do you know what is on his application?"

Silence. Dismayed, I gave her my full attention. "Did you do a check on him?"

Sloan shrugged. "It's been slow during the day, while you're at work. I have to stay entertained. No big deal." She gave me a quick grin before returning her eyes to the road. "But I think you'll be very interested to hear what I've learned."

I felt a little violated. This was my job, my coworker. But at the same time, now she had me curious as to what she had uncovered. I wavered for a moment. "Okay, fine. What did you find out?"

"Well, your boy did get his GED, that's true. But not because he had dropped out and was on the streets. It was because he was too busy cruising around the world. He was homeschooled. On his family's yacht."

I think I stopped breathing for a second as I blinked at my companion. *She can't be serious.* "Excuse me?"

"Same with that online degree. Finally popped back into the states to finish off his bachelor's on a real campus."

My mind whirled as I considered all the lies he'd told. "He made up—everything? But why would someone do something like that?"

"Who is likely to be a more interesting a choice for an internship—or for a top grad school, for that matter. A hardworking came-from-the-bottom success story, or some ultra-rich guy with everything handed to him?"

She had a point. But it was truly despicable.

"A guy like that," she continued, "he probably also did it just because he could. It has to get boring knowing you can just have whatever you want. Why not make yourself more interesting and entertain yourself at the same time?"

Now it was just disturbing. "You're able to think like a sociopath far too easily."

"Why, thank you." She flashed me a quick grin. "He's pretty clever, too. At least clever enough to restrict his imaginary criminal history to his teenage years. The records of minors are sealed. Anyway, what are you going to do about it? If you take him down, can I be there?"

What *was* I going to do about it? On the one hand, I was secretly a little ecstatic to learn my rival had skeletons. Big skeletons. But on the other . . . how would I feel if I simply won by default? I wanted real accomplishments. And as much fun as taking him down would be, I wasn't relishing being in this position. I sighed and shook my head.

"I have no idea." I focused my attention out the window, stewing in the dilemma.

When we turned a familiar corner in an unexpected direction, I glanced at my partner-in-crime. "I thought we're headed to Westbrook."

"We are. Just need to make a quick stop first."

A moment later we pulled into the parking lot of the diner. Sloan continued on to the side of the building before stopping.

I wasn't hungry after our adventures, and caffeine was the last thing I needed. "We're going to Joe's?"

"Nope. Only be a sec."

Before I could question her further, Sloan hopped out and strolled to the wall of the building, digging into her jeans pocket. Then she reached out her arm and began swiping it across the surface of the brick. A white line appeared in her hand's wake.

She was drawing, with what looked like white chalk. I watched, dumbfounded, as a graffiti-like image materialized under her direction. Standard bubble-lettering, spelling out 'DMB Forever'. She popped the chalk back in her pocket and hopped in the car, as though nothing had happened.

I blinked, waiting for an explanation. Nothing. "Um, what was that about? Are we trying to terrorize the people at Joe's, too?"

She shook her head, smiling. "No."

"So then what does 'DMB' mean?"

She started the car and turned to me. "Dave Matthews Band, of course."

My eyes widened at the absurdity. I did admit to a longtime love for the group, but tagging was definitely never part of the deal. And we were grownups. Supposedly, anyway. Was my partner a little bit crazy? There *had* been signs.

Sloan burst out laughing. "Just messing with you. It's meaningless. And it'll be washed off by rain within days. But it looks like amateur gang graffiti, so no one will pay it any attention. Except maybe the cops. They'll probably be scratching their heads wondering who the heck DMB is for quite some time."

*Oh.* "So why did you draw meaningless graffiti?"

"I need to get a message to someone. And at the moment this is the only way I can."

*Odd.* "And let me guess—you're not going to tell me who? Or what the message is?"

She gave me her annoyingly mysterious smile. "You'll know soon enough."

Maddening, this one. I sulked silently, pondering the possibilities, until we walked into our new partner Richard's office for a surprise update.

\*\*\*

Sloan was kicked back in Richard's chair, feet propped up on his desk, when the man himself waltzed through the door and froze at the sight. He stifled his initial annoyance, settling for a more conciliatory greeting with icy undertones.

"And to what do I owe the pleasure?"

I spoke up from my guest chair below him. "We're just checking in. Keeping you informed of our progress. In fixing all the trouble you've caused."

Sloan raised her eyebrows with a smile. "Like she said." She swung her feet down and moved away from the desk, gesturing grandly toward the vacated chair.

Richard huffed past her and took his seat. "Well, get on with it."

"Phase one is complete," Sloan said. "Carolyn should be plenty worked up by now. Paranoid and desperate. You've already planted your hints?"

"Yes, yes. Everything you've told me to do."

I stood. "Good. And we're on for Saturday? Your guest list is complete?"

"Done. I took care of it." Richard glared at us with disdain. "And if you don't mind, I have real work to do."

We nodded our satisfaction and turned to go. But just as we reached the door, a figure turned the corner, almost running directly into us. The woman visibly startled.

My startle was internal—when I realized the woman was Carolyn Evans.

"Oh, I apologize," she said, taking a step back. Then recognition clicked and she looked at me more closely. My stomach sank.

"Wait. Don't I know you?"

I sped through my options. No way I could get out

cleanly with denial. My face lit up with pleased recognition. "Oh yes—Mrs. Evans. So good to see you."

Richard pounced, sensing new information. He sidled up to me. "So you two know each other?"

"Why, yes," Carolyn answered. "Dr. Bailey—or should I say, soon-to-be doctor—is using our facility in her dissertation study. Should be starting very shortly, if I remember correctly." She turned to me. "Are you thinking of doing something here as well? They don't really fit the profile for noise exposure."

I nodded in answer, grateful for the hint. "I'm finding that out. But I'm just exploring some options. See if there's a need for intervention in any other types of work environments."

"Well, the ambition is admirable." She turned to Richard. "I won't keep you. I just needed that contact information you offered. The security company?"

"Sure." Richard moved quickly to his desk and located a business card in his top drawer. He flashed a look of concern when he handed it to Carolyn. "Everything okay?"

She took a deep breath and let it out before responding. "Fine. I just want to look into my options. Can't be too careful these days." She gave me a quick nod, continuing to ignore Sloan's presence. "Best of luck."

I tried to take advantage of the exit. "We should be going, too."

Richard reached for me as I moved toward the door.

"Actually, I have a few more questions if you don't mind. *Doctor Bailey.*"

I halted, paralyzed.

Carolyn raised her hand in a little wave. "See you this weekend, Richard."

I gulped as she disappeared down the hall. Satisfied she was gone, Richard moved closer, his eyes twinkling with dark pleasure.

"So who exactly do we have here?"

Sloan stepped between us, giving me a moment to get myself together. My worlds were colliding, and I didn't like the possibilities for the explosion.

"None of your concern."

Ignoring Sloan, he peered around her at me with curiosity. "You're not even an investigator, are you?"

I finally gathered my wits and went for vague. "At the moment, I'm functioning in that capacity."

He shook off Sloan by stepping to the side and gave me a direct look. "Well, it sounds like you're functioning in quite a few capacities, then."

I shrugged. "I stay busy. Has nothing to do with your situation."

"Oh, I think it might. Dissertation? Doctor? A gal like that doesn't usually get mixed up in something like this. I'd be willing to bet there's somebody above you that wouldn't be very happy to hear about all your *after-school activities.*"

"Yeah, we know all about your betting," Sloan retorted. "Doesn't sound like you're very good at it."

221

"My personal time is my business," I added. "And you wouldn't know anything about it."

"Ah, but I could." His face turned darker as he leaned in. "Listen here, sweetheart. I know your soft spot now. This whole thing doesn't go my way, I'll be sure to make it my business to bring you down, too. My secrets come out—well, so do yours."

Richard gave me a sinister grin before backing away. He returned to his desk and dismissed us with a wave. "You can go."

I maintained my poker face despite my inner uproar. We walked calmly toward the door. Unwilling to let Richard believe he had the upper hand, Sloan shot him a smug grin as we exited. "We'll be seeing you, Richard. *Real soon.*"

# TWENTY-SIX

I had no idea what I was expecting when she flipped on the light, but I still found myself pleasantly surprised. *So this is what a PI hideout looks like.* Since Richard's personal threat I'd had a few days off from the truth-seeking game, leading me to spend a little too much time in my own head with his words. So a little change was a welcome distraction.

I took in the loft space. The room was small but felt much larger due to the soaring ceiling and wall of windows. A large exposed-brick wall and subway sign art gave the space a hip urban vibe. A large black desk, antique-looking filing cabinet and funky leather chairs filled out the otherwise sparse room.

"Luckily I have my own entrance," Sloan said, "so no one keeps track of my coming and going. I'm sure it wouldn't surprise you to know I prefer my privacy."

It was the first time she'd implied there was anyone else. "So you work with other investigators?"

"Sort of. Our little shop dabbles in a few different areas. I handle most of the personal investigations, on my own, while my partner focuses on other matters. He and his employees have offices down that way." She pointed to a door at the back. "I don't see him much, mainly just check in to discuss cases. But we help each other out when we need it. It's a perfect setup."

My nod of understanding turned into a startle when a loud bang shook the window beside me. The whites of two eyes glowed from the darkness beyond the glass. Showcasing two stunning emerald irises.

Sloan raised her voice to the dark figure. "Well, it's about time!"

I tried my hardest not to stare when she unlocked the window and a dark-clad man climbed into the room. It wasn't so much the surprising entrance that had me averting my eyes self-consciously. It was the man that emerged from the hood over his head. The guy was gorgeous.

He unzipped his sweatshirt and shook it off, revealing a fitted gray t-shirt that hugged powerful biceps and a toned torso. Dark jeans clung to him in wet patches. It must've begun raining outside. I finally forced my eyes away, wanting an explanation.

Sloan appeared immune to the sight. "Well, you're just in the nick of time. We were almost going to have to find some other underground genius to help."

"Yeah, yeah," he muttered. "I'm here, aren't I?" He threw the wet hoodie onto the nearest chair and ran a hand through his damp chestnut hair. The resulting look was more disheveled and somehow even sexier.

Finally Sloan reacted to my inquisitive expression. "Quinn, this cheerful visitor is Lucas. He's going to help us set up for our little showdown this weekend."

"Showdown?" Lucas scoffed, ignoring the introductions. "What are you into now, Mack?"

"Easy now," Sloan said. "Be nice. And say hello to my friend."

Like a switch being flipped, his face transformed as he turned to me. A megawatt smile lit up his handsome face. "You're right. Nice to meet you." He exuded easy charm as he shook my hand. "Sorry. I just have a lot going on right now. And this one," he flashed a stern look at Sloan, "is always into something."

Without waiting for a response, Lucas turned and flopped into the nearest chair. Just like that, the charm had vanished. And I was invisible.

He sucked in a deep breath. "Okay, so what's up?"

Sloan perched on the edge of the desk in front of him. "We need a full-coverage surveillance spread. Hoping to close out a case. But before we get to that, what's up with the mysterious entrance? Forgotten how doors work with all your skulking around?"

"I've been keeping a low profile. There's a bit of a . . . misunderstanding."

Sloan looked only mildly concerned. "Are you in trouble?"

"Not yet, as such. There's someone I need to find, then I'll be able to clear everything up. No need to worry. Yet."

"If you say so." Sloan pulled a business card from her jeans pocket and handed it to Lucas. "Here's the address. Hope you've got plenty of cameras available—we need you to cover every inch of the place with them in the morning. Nice and discreet."

Lucas seemed unfazed by the urgent timeline. "Got it."

"But then some strategically placed fake ones, too."

*Fake cameras?* I was baffled as to why we would need them in Richard's house, but didn't want to flaunt my inexperience. I stayed invisible and listened, fascinated.

"Not a problem. What about access?"

"The owner will be expecting you," Sloan answered. "I doubt you'll find him very personable. But he'll do whatever you need, or he can answer to me."

"Ah, I see. A hostile takeover. And what exactly is the goal here?"

"Like I said, we're closing out the case. This should get us some answers. Clear up whether we're just dealing with a greedy, scheming client and a tragedy—or a true criminal conspiracy."

Lucas let out what sounded like a growl of frustration. "Why can't you just stick to background checks and pictures of cheating husbands?"

"Believe it or not, that's how this all started." Sloan ignored the hostility and looked to me with a sly smile. "We're just extra thorough."

"Fine. And the feeds—routed to your laptop?"

"With normal backup precautions, of course."

Still a little lost, but used to the feeling by now.

"Well, if that's all you have for me." Lucas hopped from his chair and moved toward the window, grabbing his sweatshirt on the way.

Sloan followed him. "You're going back out that way?"

"Unexplained things just make people ask questions. If I never came in—I can't very well be seen going out. You know that."

"Good point. So, no hints as to how to find you?"

He scratched at the dark stubble on his strong jaw as he stared back for a moment. "Better you don't know. But you know how to reach me." He raised his eyebrows, giving her a subtle smile. "Next time you might try a song title instead. Keep 'em guessing."

"Fine." She thought for a second. "How about 'I'll back you up'?"

*Ah, Dave Matthews—the mysterious chalk message.* Of course.

Lucas smirked. "Fitting enough." He reached his hand to Sloan's hair and gently tucked a lock behind her ear. His gaze was affectionate for just a brief moment. Then he turned and climbed out the window and into the night, without another word.

I watched out the window a moment, waiting to ensure privacy. Then I gave Sloan a bug-eyed stare.

She returned a blank gaze. "What?"

"Um, do you have anything to tell me?"

Sloan's quizzical look was clearly faked. "Like?"

"Like—who exactly was that? Are you dating?"

"Oh. Gross." She scowled and flipped open the laptop on the desk. "No."

"Gross!" *Um, no.* "I don't know who you saw, but that's hardly the word I'd use to describe the god that was just in here. Gruff, maybe. But definitely not gross."

Sloan focused her attention on the computer, ignoring me. I wasn't going to let her off that easily.

Finally she sighed. "Okay, look. You're right. Luke is tall and dark and handsome and brilliant—and pretty much everything one could want." She looked up, finally meeting my eyes. "Just like his brother. Joel."

*Oh.*

She shrugged. "They were practically twins. Barely more than a year apart and best friends."

"So that explains his protectiveness? He was like family?"

Sloan nodded, her mind elsewhere. "He still is." She looked back at me again. "And so no, I definitely don't have any feelings for Lucas. That would be way too weird. Incestuous."

I was fascinated by the subtle relief I felt at her declaration. Brusque men that ignore me were not usually my thing. But I guess my 'thing' had been a little all over the map lately.

"But wait a minute," Sloan said, amusement taking over her face. "I think maybe *you* have a thing for Lucas."

I scoffed. "Right."

"Liar. And he's just your type. Dark hair, light eyes, brainiac."

"Don't forget surly," I shot back. "Tough guys are your thing, remember?"

"Nah, don't let him fool you. It's just an act. He's actually very thoughtful and sensitive if you get to know him." She closed the laptop. "He's just frustrated he can't keep me from doing my job. After his brother, he's been trying to keep me away from trouble. Unsuccessfully, of course. It's sweet, really."

"Well, regardless, he barely acknowledged my existence. I don't think you need to worry about a love connection."

"I'm not worried. In fact, I think it would be a great idea for you to get out there. But I should warn you not to get too close."

"I have zero interest in getting too close, trust me." I tried to let it go, but my curiosity got the best of me. I did my best to sound nonchalant. "But why, exactly?"

Sloan began gathering her things. "Let's just say I don't take him as the settling down type. And I seriously suspect you are. So you'd have to keep that in mind, should you ever get to know him."

"Whatever," I said breezily. But I wasn't sure what to make of her statement. I didn't like being pigeonholed.

Really, who could know what type I was? I certainly didn't seem to anymore.

I shook it off. "What's he do, anyway? Why is he hiding out?"

"I'll have to let him fill you in sometime. It's . . . complicated." Sloan moved to open the door. "Anyway, looks like our job is done for now. My sources tell me Carolyn has been terrorized enough that she's hired a personal security team, so she's primed and ready. I'm glad you weren't permanently scared off by Richard's threats. Still with me, right?"

I thought about it one last time as I followed her out. Even after all my stress over how my boss could react to me playing spy in my free time, there was no way I was going to let him intimidate me into backing down now. We'd come too far. "Yep. I'm good."

"Smart girl." She flipped off the lights and pulled the door behind us. The old building was deserted after hours. "Get some good sleep tonight, because we have a very special party to go to tomorrow. I think it'll be *quite* enlightening."

# TWENTY-SEVEN

The lying in wait looks so much more exciting in the movies.

Here in Blaine's sports-themed childhood bedroom, anxiously counting down to our big moment, I was too on edge to use the time to read research articles as I had hoped. Instead I kept checking each camera view on the laptop, obsessively making sure each was working. So much for being productive in other parts of my life. But finally Richard's party downstairs was getting into swing and there was something to watch on the video feed.

I looked over at Sloan. Legs thrown casually across the side of the armchair, she was leisurely reading a novel as though she had no worries in the world. As though she were involved in a sting operation to ensnare a possible murder-for-hire client everyday. Who knew, maybe she was.

But her annoying nonchalance did make me feel better. She didn't seem too concerned.

As the gathering on the main floor grew, I focused on the view of the front door. The great room was full of middle-aged professionals. Mostly business acquaintances, I assumed. Surely a man like Richard didn't have this many *actual* friends. Our guest of honor was casually late.

I couldn't stay quiet any longer. "What if she doesn't show up?"

Sloan didn't look up from her book. "Don't worry, she'll show."

I gritted my teeth nervously and checked all the cameras one more time. *Wait. There she is!*

Carolyn Evans had just walked in the door, wearing a solemn black dress and heels. She was accompanied by a handsome dark-skinned man with a shaved head. He was dressed in all black, just like the two equally strong-looking men that tailed them in. She had clearly brought her new security team.

I must have gasped involuntarily, because Sloan swung her legs off the chair and hopped onto the bed next to me, abandoning her novel.

"Here we go," she said. "Well, almost. We have to let her settle in a bit first. Looks like she's nice and paranoid. That's a good start."

To my chagrin, I was still in the dark about some of the plan. Sloan seemed to enjoy unveiling information about her scheme a little bit at a time. I tried to pry out a little more. "So how is Richard getting her away from the party, exactly?"

Sloan smiled mischievously. "There's going to be another special delivery, but this time for Richard, and much scarier. She'll talk once she sees this one."

Sloan stretched out on her stomach beside me. I stayed sitting cross-legged, eyes focused on the screen. We both watched in silence for a while. It was easy to follow Carolyn visually as she small-talked her way through the crowd. We wouldn't need to use the sound until things started to happen.

By the time Carolyn made it to the bar, we had noticed the host make multiple trips to the bartender. Richard caught up with her there and ordered another drink.

"He better not get too drunk to pull this off." There was a little worry in Sloan's voice for the first time.

While the pair was engrossed in what looked like a friendly conversation, someone carried in an oversized gift-wrapped item and placed it on a table near Richard.

Sloan sat up suddenly. "It's here. Turn on the sound."

Party guests paused to check out the basket-shaped object with a dramatically large red bow. We watched as Richard approached the basket warily. Carolyn wandered away in the meantime.

"Don't go too far," Sloan teased to the screen.

Someone in the crowd called out for Richard to see who sent the gift. He opened the card and reluctantly read aloud. "To Richard. Best wishes on your big deal coming up. I hope to share with you in your company's prosperous future. No signature."

The watching crowd tittered and urged him to open the package. Richard carefully untied the bow and removed the layers of opaque cellophane. Before we could get a good view, a woman's shriek rang out from below us. And then another.

The crowd backed away from the sight and I got my first look. There was a child's doll dangling from the handle of the basket. Twine was roped around the doll's neck and tied at the side, causing the doll to list eerily to the side as it swayed. The open, staring eyes had small X marks across them in black marker. Tiny paper headstones marked RIP were planted in the basket's red paper lining. The party guests gaped at the disturbing diorama.

Richard recovered from the sight quickly and retrieved the manila envelope peeking from underneath the basket.

"Don't worry, everyone," he called out. "I'm sure there's an explanation for this." He moved away from the crowd before opening the envelope. His expression was blank as he examined the contents and reclosed the packet. Then a smile split his face.

"Just my son's strange sense of humor." There were gasps in the crowd. "I told him he has to stop playing around and get a real job working for me. I guess he didn't appreciate that very much. He always has loved Halloween. Can you still ground a twenty-six year old?"

Richard waited for a few chuckles and groans before finishing. "Someone come get rid of this nonsense. Enjoy the party everybody."

The crowd began chattering loudly. Richard made his way through the crowd, ignoring the guests patting and clapping his shoulders in solidarity as he passed. He headed straight for Carolyn Evans.

Sloan startled me when she spoke again. "He's a much better actor than I would've guessed. Show time."

\*\*\*

It was only a minute before they passed our hiding spot and appeared on the video feed from Richard's study. He slammed the door shut.

"Richard, tell me what is this all about," Carolyn demanded.

"No, I think you need to tell *me* what this is about," he replied. "What have you gotten me into?"

She spat her words right back. "What are you talking about?"

"I'm talking about this." Richard dumped the contents of the manila envelope on the desk. A small baggy of white powder landed on top of a stack of photographs.

Carolyn moved closer to get a look. "What is this?" She slid the bag aside and picked up the top photograph. I recognized it as one of Sloan's from the hotel bar. "This is Carter. What is the meaning of this?"

"It came with the friendly gift you saw delivered. Check the back."

She flipped it over and read the message scrawled in

permanent marker. *At least he enjoyed his last night. Thought you might want his last photo.*

Carolyn gasped in horror and threw the picture on the desk. She glared at Richard, who stood fuming, saying nothing. Then her eyes caught on the rest of the stack still sitting untouched.

She moved closer and picked the first one up, hesitant. I could make out Carolyn, sitting alone at a table, looking off to the side. It was taken from a distance. She turned the picture over, her hands now visibly shaking. There was another message: *You didn't say cheese.*

Carolyn gaped at Richard. Stone-faced, he picked up the third and final photo and thrust it at her. This one was a shot of an unsuspecting Richard, getting into his car. She studied it and turned it over. I could see her chest heaving as her breathing accelerated. Richard moved to a mini-bar in the corner and began refilling his drink with a dark liquor on ice.

Carolyn read the final message out loud. "'I want in. Take on a new business partner—and you and your secrets are safe. See you soon.' What the hell does this mean?"

Richard gulped from his glass before responding bitterly. "You know what it means. We're being blackmailed."

"By the man that you sent me to? Who did you put us in bed with, Richard?"

"It was sent by the man I told you to have a simple conversation about narcotics with," he replied. "You were supposed to get some drugs from him, to make our lives easier. Obviously something more happened, because Carter is dead." Richard stabbed at the photo in her hands in fury. "And now this. Tell me what happened."

"That's all. That's all that happened." Carolyn was indignant.

"That doesn't make any sense." He drank more of his drink and glared at Carolyn. She glared back.

"Fine," he said finally. "Then we need to call the police."

"Absolutely not."

"I'm not going to be terrorized by some thug that thinks he can hold our companies hostage." His voice was angry. "We tell the police what happened, and then there's nothing to blackmail us with."

"No," Carolyn repeated, shaking her head. "We can't."

"You can handle the slap on the wrist for the drugs. Your lawyers will get you out of that, you know that. But we had nothing to do with your husband. Buying the drugs doesn't make you at fault, even if we did have dishonorable intentions."

"There has to be another way—" Carolyn was beginning to sound a little desperate.

Richard walked to the desk. "You saw that thing they sent. I can't take any chances. I'm calling." He picked up the receiver and began to dial.

Carolyn rushed forward and slammed down the hook switch, disconnecting the call. She looked up at him gravely, no longer seeming scared. "You don't understand. We. Can't. Go. To the police."

Richard tensed and let his hand drop to his side. The dial tone was still audible while he stared, unmoving. His face was hardened with fury when he finally spoke. "Tell me why not right now, or I'm calling."

Carolyn stared back, appraising. After a moment she let out a breath and her shoulders dropped in resignation. But before she could speak, her eyes shot to the corners of the room, scanning. She spotted the small fake camera planted in the corner opposite our real one.

She turned to Richard, aghast. "You have security cameras in your house?"

"A few."

Carolyn gathered her thoughts for a moment before calling out for her security detail waiting in the hallway. The lead guy rushed through the door.

"Take his phone," she ordered. "And check him for a wire."

"Carolyn, you're being paranoid."

"Do you want me to talk to you or not? We're moving somewhere more private."

Richard didn't argue with the lethal-looking man that approached. He handed over his phone and allowed himself to be patted down. Carolyn disappeared from the study for a moment.

Richard had just been cleared when she reappeared in the doorway and glared at him. "Follow me."

# TWENTY-EIGHT

Sloan looked ready to burst with excitement. "It's working. I wonder which room is going to make her feel secure enough to spill her guts?"

I finally understood the reason for the fake camera. *Let her think she's outsmarted the system.* I had a lot to learn.

We watched the camera feed, enthralled. Carolyn led him through the master bedroom and into the attached walk-in closet. The room lined with dark custom cabinets was twice the size of my bedroom.

Richard scoffed when they entered the room. "My closet?"

"I can't imagine you worried about the maid stealing your sweaty suits, so yes. I'll talk in here. After you take off your clothes." Before he could object, she held up her hand obstinately. "I'm not taking any chances. You can hand over your suit, or I'm leaving. Now."

Richard's face turned red with outrage, but he began yanking off his clothing. He threw the items in a pile on the floor. When he was down to white boxer shorts and black dress socks, Carolyn raised her hand again.

"That's enough," she said, grimacing. "I don't need to see any more."

"Fine. Now what the hell have you gotten me into?"

Carolyn waited until the bodyguard gathered the discarded clothing and exited the room, closing the door behind him.

"I don't know," she began. She wandered a moment distractedly, as though gathering her thoughts. "It never occurred to me that someone like that would have the wherewithal to plan an extortion like this." Her look of distress seemed genuine when she looked up at Richard. "I need your help."

Richard's face softened just a little. "Tell me what happened."

"I went to see your guy to get a little something to plant on Carter, just as we planned."

"As you planned," Richard interrupted. "I merely suggested. I was just brainstorming."

"Whatever. I went to him, and somehow I ended up telling him what I needed it for." Carolyn shook her head, as though frustrated by the memory. "I never bought any drugs. He asked a lot of questions. Then he sort of—suggested—that he could make sure that my husband used, and partied a little too hard. I . . . agreed. And paid him."

Richard's eyes narrowed. "What does that mean, exactly?"

"I don't know," she replied quickly. "I mean, I assumed it meant just that . . . that he would ensure that Carter had too much. Maybe he would have to be taken to the hospital. He'd never be able to get his job back then."

She paused and looked up at Richard gravely. "But I guess a part of me knew he could mean something more serious. So I wasn't all that surprised when I learned that Carter was dead. But I never asked what he meant— because I didn't want to know."

My mouth dropped open. I couldn't believe it had worked. She may not have overtly requested murder, but she had clearly allowed it to be implied.

I looked to Sloan. Her eyes twinkled with delight. "Gotcha."

Back on the screen, Richard continued playing his part well. He stared at the woman in shock. "Whether you knew what he was going to do or not—you basically paid him to get rid of your husband. Is that what you're telling me?"

"It could be interpreted that way." Her voice was careful. "But I never actually said it, and there's no proof. It's the word of this shady character against mine."

"It doesn't matter," Richard retorted. "If even a hint of this gets out, your business is finished. And now you've brought me into this."

"You sent me to that criminal in the first place, Richard. So really, this is all your fault." Carolyn visibly stiffened and regarded Richard carefully. "Actually, how do I know you aren't behind this whole thing?"

"What the hell are you talking about?" Richard's eyes flamed with fury.

"You're the reason I ever got involved with those people in the first place. I know about your gambling debts. He told me *all* about your issues." She stalked closer, staring him down. "Who's to say you didn't set me up? Give him a nice, easy way to make some money on blackmail. While he, what? Reduces your debt, perhaps?"

"That's preposterous." Richard glowered down at her, their faces now inches apart. "Even if I wanted to do something like that—don't you think I know it would blow up in my face? I'd be drug into this just as much as you."

Carolyn held his glare, considering. Finally her shoulders relaxed in a sigh. "Fine." She backed away, easing the visible tension between them. "Well, then what are we going to do about this? We can't possibly make that *thug* a partner."

Richard shook his head emphatically. "No. Unacceptable." He stared off in the distance, pondering, before returning his attention to his co-conspirator. "Maybe we can buy him off another way. Now that there's nothing in the way, if we can finally get this deal through then you and I can put together a nice payoff without having to get him anywhere near our business."

Carolyn grimaced. "It makes me sick that we'd give into this scum. And rats like that have a way of sticking around. They show back up wanting more."

"We'll just have to deal with that if it comes to it. I don't see any other way."

Carolyn looked like she wanted to argue, but held back. She let out another sigh. "I think you're right. Okay."

Richard looked relieved, sensing his job was done. "We'll have to look at the numbers on Monday and figure something out. In the meantime, I have a houseful of people downstairs."

Carolyn looked just as relieved. "Right. I'll have them bring back your clothes."

"Don't bother. I've got more."

Carolyn nodded her head and left the room without another word. We watched her head back down to the party, her security team at her heels. Richard yanked down a new suit and redressed quickly.

\*\*\*

He did not return to the party immediately. Once fully clothed, Richard headed straight back to his study and fixed himself a tall drink. He looked mentally and emotionally exhausted. We took the opportunity to break from our vigilance while he was decompressing.

"That was amazing," I said, beaming.

Sloan grinned at me. "Fun, wasn't it?"

"Absolutely."

"How about some champagne, then? I swiped an open

bottle before the party." Sloan moved to the dresser, where two glasses and a bottle on ice were waiting.

I couldn't believe I was a part of this. Just yesterday I was having a normal day at the office. And today I was helping coax a conspiracy confession from a prominent businesswoman. *Wait—is my role in this going to get out?*

Sloan saw the concern creeping onto my face when she handed me a glass. "What is it?"

"Well, it's just . . . " I hesitated, unsure. "Is my work going to find out about me doing this? I'm not sure they would approve of a side job tricking criminals."

"I don't see why they have to. I'll turn the recordings into the police—that should be all they need. I doubt I'll even have to bring your name into it. And Carolyn never even knew you were here."

"That's true." I nodded, feeling better. "And so there's no reason it should affect my research project, whether she's around or not."

"I wouldn't imagine. So let's celebrate a job well done, secret side job or not."

We clinked glasses and took a sip. I glanced at the video feed of Richard in his office. He was starting on what must've been a newly freshened drink, pacing around in silence.

Suddenly I heard a low grumbling from the laptop speaker. "Wait, turn it up."

Sloan increased the volume. There was nothing again.

Then the sound of Richard slamming his emptied glass on the desk.

When he finally spoke again, his speech was beginning to slur. "Do you hear me? I'm done. You people better have gotten everything you need, because I'm not doing another damn thing."

I turned to Sloan. "We need to stop him. What if someone hears him?"

"We can't go out there and take a chance on being seen."

Richard's voice boomed from the laptop. "And all these cameras better be out of my house as soon as the party's over, or I'm smashing them all myself. I don't appreciate being pushed around and setting up my friends. To hell with your plan."

Suddenly another voice appeared. "What are you talking about, Richard?"

In the corner of the video feed we finally noticed Carolyn, standing in the study doorway. *We didn't kept an eye out for her.* I looked to Sloan in panic. She was frozen, spellbound by the scene.

Richard slowly turned toward the door. He seemed to take a moment to process her presence before he stiffened. "What? Nothing," he muttered.

Carolyn stalked closer. "Setting up your friends? What plan?"

"I don't know what you're talking about. I need to get back to the party." He attempted to brush past her, but she stopped him with a hand on his chest.

"I heard you, Richard." Carolyn's voice became soothing, as if talking to a child. "But there's no one here. Who were you talking to?"

"No one. I don't know what you're talking about."

Carolyn's eyes searched the corners of the room again before resuming her smooth tone. "I came back to retrieve those blackmail photos—and I heard it all. I know someone must be listening. Does that mean you tricked me into talking about what happened?"

Richard didn't respond. He glared at the floor.

"Would you do that to me, Richard?"

He tipped his empty glass to his mouth, still ignoring her.

When she spoke again, her honeyed voice was replaced by the sound of wrath. "You listen to me. I will ruin you. I will go downstairs and tell your guests *all* your sordid secrets. And I know about a lot more than just the gambling." She poked her finger into his chest as she spoke. "Is. There. Someone. Listening."

Richard looked briefly up at her, a defeated look on his unfocused face. His only response was an almost imperceptible nod. He returned his focus to the carpet.

Carolyn's breathing became audible as she glared at Richard in fury. We gaped at the screen. Before we could react, she called out to her security detail waiting in the hallway. They burst into the study.

"Search this house, it's bugged," she ordered. "Someone here is trying to set me up."

# TWENTY-NINE

I turned to Sloan in panic, heart racing. I saw a glimpse of the same alarm in her face before she quickly recovered. "Don't worry, the door is locked," she whispered.

A moment later we heard the door handle rattle vigorously, then stop. I felt my shoulders sag in relief when the hallway went quiet again.

BAM! The door flew open and banged loudly against the wall, a black combat boot propelling it. The attached body of the lead bodyguard continued into the room and quickly assessed the situation with wild eyes.

Before I could react with anything other than terror, he slammed the laptop shut in front of me and yanked it away. He studied us momentarily. Then I heard his voice for the first time as he called out to his other men.

"Bring them in."

I looked quickly at Sloan. Her eyes looked as wide as mine, and I was not reassured this time.

Two bodyguards stepped in from behind and approached. I was too terrified to resist when one grabbed my arm. As they led us down the hallway, it occurred to me that there was a party full of guests downstairs. *I could just scream for help.*

Sloan seemed to read my mind before I could act. "Just do as they say." She gave me an earnest look. I decided to trust her judgement, despite my reservations.

As we entered the study, I heard the lead bodyguard on the stairs, telling guests at the bottom not to worry, that there was just a little mishap upstairs. A moment later he entered the room behind us carrying the seized laptop. He closed the study door, standing guard.

"You," Carolyn spat when she saw me. "What do you have to do with this?"

I opened my mouth to speak, but nothing came out. I was frozen.

She pounced again. "What is this, corporate espionage? Who are you working for?"

I still hadn't quite found my words when Sloan spoke up. "No, Richard here hired us, believe it or not."

Carolyn turned her glare on Sloan. To my amazement, Sloan had already regained her cool.

"Well, he hired *me*, anyway," she continued. "But his devious plans kind of backfired on him, and here we are."

Carolyn's head whipped to face Richard. "What is going on? Who are these people, and why do you have them here?"

He continued to stare at the floor, sullen. He took another gulp of his drink, swaying a little as he did.

Once again Sloan took the lead. "I can clear a few things up, since he seems a little indisposed at the moment."

Carolyn turned back to appraise Sloan. I would have withered under her icy gaze.

Sloan gazed back confidently. "We're here to get to the truth of what happened to your husband. If it really had been an accident, no problem. We would've gone on our way. But you were kind enough to explain what really happened."

Standing in the room full of hired muscle, I was baffled by Sloan's fearlessness. I had trusted she would make up a story. Instead she seemed to be making it worse. *Hope she knows what she's doing.*

She continued. "It may not have been your idea, but you went along with it. Even if it's not murder, that's gotta be worth at least a conspiracy charge."

Carolyn glared back. "And you have a tape of our conversation?"

"Actually, we do. But I'm guessing if you cooperate and help bring in the thug who did do it, they'll go easy on you."

"You two aren't cops.".

"Nope," Sloan responded. "Just interested parties."

The woman paused, considering. Then her face hardened in determination as she looked at us. "Then there's nothing you can do, really." She reached to her purse beside her on the desk. Before I could process what she was doing, she pulled out a small silver pistol.

She pointed it coldly at Sloan.

Everyone tensed in surprise. The lead bodyguard moved forward a fraction.

"Hold up," he said, holding his hands in the air. "Easy now. What are you doing with that?"

"Just getting this under control." Carolyn's eyes were locked on Sloan. "Give me the laptop."

The man complied, slowly placing it on the desk next to her. He stayed close, watching intently.

Carolyn lifted the computer screen with her free hand, then grabbed Richard's open bottle of scotch from the desktop and poured the remaining contents onto the keyboard. *Was all of this for nothing?* But we had bigger problems, with a gun pointed at Sloan and a room full of presumably armed men of unknown persuasion.

The bodyguard spoke calmly. "You have the laptop. So why don't you put the gun down and let us handle it from here?"

She sneered at his request. "And exactly how are you going to handle it? They can still talk, even without the recording."

"That's true, that's true. But I'm sure we can work something out."

She was breathing heavily, clearly unsure what to do next. Her eyes looked wildly between the occupants of the room. I glanced at Sloan. She was glaring fiercely at the woman pointing a gun at her.

Carolyn returned Sloan's gaze and her resolve seemed to return. She directed her voice to the side. "Your contract indicated that you handle sensitive problems discreetly."

The bodyguard shifted closer. "Yes, that's right."

She took a deep breath and narrowed her eyes at Sloan before she spoke again. "So do you make problems *go away?*"

Everyone paused while her words hung in the air. Her meaning was clear. My stomach dropped. *Surely the security guards won't go along with her.*

"Not officially," the bodyguard replied carefully, inching closer. "But why don't we go talk in private, see what we can work out. My guys can handle this for now."

I was starting to feel lightheaded from my racing pulse. I needed to think of something, and quickly. I thought back to my lessons in deception so far. *When in doubt, bluff.* I had no idea how to apply that at the moment.

Vaguely I heard a buzz from beside me. Sloan's phone was vibrating. Suddenly I had an idea, and before I could stop to fully consider it, I heard my voice ring out.

"I think you'll want her to get that."

Sloan gave me a fleeting look of confusion before pulling out the buzzing phone. The screen read 'Lucas'. *That'll work.*

"The video was automatically uploaded to our boss

every few seconds." I was making it up on the fly. "He already has it. If he can't reach us, he'll send the recording straight to the police."

Unfortunately, I didn't exactly have a plan beyond this point. Just a vague hope that Sloan could get a coded message to Lucas, and maybe buy us some time.

The phone continued to vibrate. The woman began to look panicked as we all stared, waiting.

"Answer it," Carolyn finally ordered. She shot Sloan a disturbing forced smile. "Tell him everything's just fine, and maybe we can *all* work out a deal."

Sloan smirked smugly in return. "Okay." She punched the answer button on the phone. "Hey Lucas." She stared directly at Carolyn. "Yeah, send the police. Now."

*No!*

Carolyn's face contorted with rage. I watched in slow motion as she lifted the gun higher and pulled the trigger, mere feet from Sloan's chest.

I was instantly disoriented by the blast, my ringing ears blurring my perception. The lead bodyguard immediately tackled Carolyn to the ground. The gun bounced quietly across the carpet. The other two men rushed past me to help.

I finally recovered my bearings enough to turn and check on my friend. Sloan lifted her eyes from the skirmish and grinned. She was still standing next to me, seemingly unharmed. No blood, no bullet holes. I was baffled but relieved beyond belief.

"How?" It was all I could manage at that point.

"It was a blank." Sloan's smile turned apologetic. "Sorry we had to scare you."

***

An hour later, I was finally released from questioning by the police. We had all been separated to give our individual accounts of the situation. I explained everything I knew—which was clearly not the whole story. The officer interrogating me was not inclined fill me in. I went in search of Sloan to get the rest of the story, relief and confusion battling inside.

I found her down the hall, back in the study. I subconsciously still expected to find crime scene tape and a chalk outline. But no violence had occurred here.

Sloan gave me a sympathetic smile when she saw me. "There's someone I need to introduce you to. Quinn, meet Hudson." She gestured at the lead security guard next to her. "My business partner."

My eyes widened as the man stepped forward. His smile was kind as he shook my hand with an arm that looked beyond lethal.

"Nice to finally meet you," he said. "I've heard a lot about you."

"And yet I've heard nothing about you." I flashed Sloan a confused look.

She looked sheepish in return. "He runs our security

consulting division. Please don't be mad at me. If it helps, you played your part perfectly. You couldn't have set up the ending any better if you tried."

"My part?" The initial shock was beginning to morph into annoyance. Clearly I had been used in some way. "Which was what, exactly?"

"Just to be scared, that's all," Sloan said calmly. "I couldn't fill you in on the fact that the security team was on our side. I didn't know just how good of an actress you were yet. I'm not sure you know yourself. So I was trying to make it easier on you—by making it harder, if that makes any sense."

*Sloan and her surprises.* I guessed it did make sense, but I wasn't going to tell her that. I would have to think this deception through later. "So this was all planned? Making me think we were going to be shot?"

Sloan shook her head. "All we planned was recording the confession. But since we weren't sure who we were dealing with, making sure she hired our security team to keep on eye on things seemed like the smart thing to do. Which was definitely helpful when Carolyn decided to begin carrying a weapon."

I looked at Hudson. "So you, what, switched out the bullets in the gun?"

He smiled. "Swapped her entire box for blanks. And double checked it every move we made. She never had any real power."

"Which is why you had no problem provoking her," I said to Sloan.

She shrugged. "Might as well push her and see what happens. Now we know what she's really capable of."

With the adrenaline wearing off, attempting to contemplate the dangerous situation we had been a part of only made my head swim.

"It's a lot to process, I know," Sloan said. "But I feel good about taking someone like that off the streets. And you were brave, stepping in like that. It would've been a good move. You're quick on your feet when it counts. I hope our little ruse doesn't turn you off this business for good."

I knew I shouldn't make any sweeping declarations in that moment. But with the way I was feeling in the aftermath, I had doubts about my participation in such activities in the future. I was angry at the deception, relieved at the lack of dying, and overjoyed by the sleuthing success. I had helped bring in a conspirator that had the potential to be a dangerous criminal. And I was emotionally exhausted. All I wanted to ponder at the moment was a glass of wine and a long, hot bath.

Sloan seemed to read my mind. She threw her arm around my shoulders and began to lead me out of the house. The few police remaining nodded their appreciation as we exited.

"I've got a giant bottle of moscato with your name on it. You've earned it."

# THIRTY

I had only one day to recover before the next big event. Presentation day. The competition for the opening move of my career. Sloan had tried to convince me it was the perfect opportunity. Roll out my intel and take Grant down on the spot. But at some point in the process of facing down another quasi-evil manipulator at what I thought was real gunpoint, I had decided I would have to do it my way.

I had taken her advice in another area, though. And it showed on Grant's face as soon as I walked into the office.

"What the—?" He looked me over with widened eyes. After lingering on my skinny heels, he straightened and swapped his shocked face for a saccharine smile. "Aren't you cute, with your big-girl outfit. You almost look like a grown-up professional. I just hope you don't trip and fall in those shoes, bless your heart."

I did have to admit, the shoes were impractical for

everyday wear. But it wasn't every day I was going to kick his slimy, lying ass. I ignored his futile jab and turned to the back wall mirror, where we normally checked our teeth before seeing patients after lunch. Today I used it to appraise my new look, as he pretended not to watch.

This time wasn't Sloan's handiwork. It was all mine. But I thought she would be proud. My new sleek black suit was stylish and perfectly fitted. Between the high heels and hems tailored to just a hair above the floor, I looked and felt taller than I ever had before. But the coup de grâce was my face. After I mimicked Sloan's makeup procedures, with some adjustments for workplace modesty, the aqua top peeking out of my suit made my blue eyes absolutely pop. Of course, some of the vividness probably came from the extra sparkle of seeing my co-worker's discomfort.

I smoothed a section of my shiny, newly-layered hair and turned back to Grant. "I'll be fine. I'd worry about myself, if I were you."

He stood and moved closer. His gaze was annoyed but wary, as if trying to figure me out anew. "And what is that supposed to mean?"

I gave him a direct look in return. "It means I know who you really are."

A shadow passed his eyes momentarily, but he said nothing.

"Don't worry, it's not my secret to tell. But these things always have a way of coming out eventually. So you might decide to be a little nicer to the people around you in the meantime. But I guess, until then—best of luck. We better get in there."

I grabbed my things and strolled down the hall, leaving Grant alone in the office to process my words. My future awaited, and it was no longer going to include worrying about my hypercritical coworker or trying to blend in with the background. I waltzed into the conference room with newfound confidence. And received just the reaction I had been hoping for.

\*\*\*

I like to think I looked peaceful—Zen-like, even—the moment my ankle wrenched sideways and left me sprawled across the ground.

No, thankfully, it was not during my big presentation. I had successfully made it out alive and was a bit lost in my thoughts, too busy thinking about the results of the meeting to notice the giant crack in the sidewalk behind the downtown bar that evening. As I lifted my face from the concrete I was mortified I was still such a rookie at heels, but grateful my fall appeared to have been without witnesses.

"Quinn?"

*No way. Please, no way.*

I was pretty sure I recognized the male voice behind me. I pushed myself to a sitting position before looking up to verify. Yep, it was Lucas. Looking delicious in a leather motorcycle jacket.

He rushed forward when our eyes met, all masculine concern. "You okay?"

I looked away, embarrassed. I focused on brushing the gravel from my palms. "I'll be fine." My new suit was not so fresh-looking, either. I knocked debris from my pants and jacket.

"You're a mess." Lucas held out his hand. "Here, let's get you up."

I sucked up whatever dignity I had left to spit out my response. "I'm fine, thanks." I ignored his hand and scrambled back to my full heel-enhanced height with as much grace as I could muster. I gave a final swipe across the dusty fabric of my jacket before I met his eyes again.

His head tilted a bit as he looked back at me. "You look ... different."

"I'm shocked you could notice." And I was surprised at my own tone. *What did I care?* I didn't need to take my embarrassment out on this guy. I quickly changed the subject, averting my eyes again. "What are you doing here, anyway?"

"I knew you guys were going to be here." Thankfully, he ignored my snide comment. "I hoped maybe Sloan would be early—I wanted to say goodbye. But I have to get going."

"Goodbye?" I met his eyes again, hoping mine didn't

betray the subtle stab of disappointment I felt somewhere deep inside.

"For now. Don't know how long. Have to take care of something." He stuck his hands in his pockets and regarded me carefully. "Tell her I'm sorry I won't be around to back her up for a while."

"Sure, no problem."

He paused for a moment, his naturally intense gaze turned up a notch. "And I'm sorry I won't be around to get to know you, either. Dig the look, by the way."

"Um. Sure, I'll let her know," I stammered inanely.

Lucas visibly repressed his amusement. "Well, anyway. I'm glad everything turned out okay. I'll see ya, buttercup." Without waiting for a response, he turned and crossed the parking lot to throw his leg over a waiting motorcycle.

*Buttercup!* And of course he drove a motorcycle. I hated motorcycles.

So why did I find myself turning back, trying to catch a glimpse of him roaring away? Sometimes I truly baffled myself.

I had only been nursing my drink a few minutes at a high-top when Sloan appeared, carrying a basket of some sort. She stopped to get a drink on the way, leaving the basket up front with Blaine.

She eyed the bottle and glasses on the table as she

approached. "Is that champagne I see? Does that mean what I think it means?"

I couldn't help my grin.

She gave me an excited hug before sliding onto her stool. "Tell me everything."

I gave her a rundown of how Grant had apparently been so shaken by the fact that he'd been found out—that he made a complete mess of his presentation. Stammered nervously, forgot key information, and was just all around terrible. "He even accidentally called our boss his behind-her-back nickname for her. Dr. Me Bore."

Sloan gasped and we both broke into a fit of laughter.

"Turns out I didn't need to rat him out," I finished. "I just needed to let loose his own guilt and get out of the way.

"So you got it?"

"I nailed it. And a while later they called me in for a meeting—and offered me the position. As soon as my fellowship is complete, I'll be joining the faculty."

"Congratulations!"

As I poured her a glass of the champagne, Hannah strolled through the door. She headed straight for us, without a glance toward the bar.

But she definitely didn't escape Blaine's notice. His eyes followed her to our table, his look of befuddlement deepening as she hopped onto one of our stools. I had a feeling he was intrigued as to what Hannah would be doing with us.

"Celebrating, I see," she said. "I take it you got the job?"

"I did." Elated, I handed her a glass.

"Fantastic. I have my own celebrating to do, too."

Sloan smirked. "Celebrating kicking Blaine to the curb, are we?"

We all glanced toward the bar. Blaine quickly looked away and pretended to be engrossed in a task.

"Well, that too," Hannah said, grinning. "But I also got a new job. Walter is now the sole head of the firm, and he's made me his executive assistant. With a raise. And best of all, Malibu Barbie is out of there."

We both congratulated Hannah. I glanced back toward the bar just in time to see Blaine pull something from Sloan's basket and toss it discreetly into his mouth.

I nodded my head toward the bar. "What's with the basket you brought in?"

Sloan returned a playful grin. "That, ladies, was our grand finale."

Hannah and I exchanged a puzzled look.

Sloan motioned to Hannah. "One of the things you mentioned about Blaine was that he had a major weakness for anything chocolate-peanut butter."

Hannah nodded. "Total addict. Can't help himself if it's around."

"Exactly. So I've, sort of, been bringing by a basket of the addictive little balls Sayid makes at the diner. And leaving them next to Blaine whenever he's on duty. He thinks he's doing a favor for me, advertising my homemade chocolate business."

*Uh oh.* "But really you are . . . "

Sloan smirked. "Getting back at a lying two-timing flirt by fattening him up. He can't keep his grubby little hands off 'em. He's eaten half the basket since we got here."

We all glanced over again to see Blaine pull his hand from the basket and push the whole thing down the bar, away from himself.

Hannah gaped. "I knew he'd been putting on pounds. You're so bad!"

Sloan shrugged. "Just doing women everywhere a favor. That should slow down his game a little bit, for a while anyway. But that's the last of my chocolate torture. I'll cut him loose after today."

Hannah giggled and raised her glass. "I'll cheers to that."

"Congratulations all around then." Sloan raised hers.

I lifted my glass and looked to Sloan. "So what are you celebrating? Solving the mystery?"

"Sure, bringing someone to justice is reward in itself. As long as I get paid." Her playful face turned serious as she turned to me. "But I'm also celebrating what I hope is a new partnership. I know you have a real career and all, but I think we make a great team. I couldn't have done this without you. And I've had more fun in the past few weeks than I ever have."

I couldn't disagree. I smiled back. "Cheers, indeed."

We all clinked glasses and took sips. Then gulps, broken by laughter.

I suddenly had a thought. "So what made you think you might want to bring me into all this in the first place?"

She smiled back at me warmly. "I usually get paid for my investigations, but it's just a job. So let's just say . . . I guess I wanted to check out a real-life mystery instead."

I felt myself reddening a little at the memory of my own stumbling words. I mentally blamed it on the champagne.

"So next time I have something interesting," she continued, "does that mean I give you a call?"

I tried my best to hide my grin. "We'll just have to see when you come up with something, won't we?"

###

# ABOUT THE AUTHOR

Carrie Ann Knox is an audiologist, writer, and longtime mystery lover. After finishing a clinical doctorate and opening her own practice, she began to indulge her other passion, crafting stories that appeal to those with a thirst for adventure, technology and mystery. She also enjoys curling up with her dog Gizmo and a good book in their home in southeast Virginia.

\*\*\*

# Want to continue the SONIC SLEUTHS ADVENTURES?
## Sign up for updates & Connect with Carrie Ann!

 www.CarrieAnnKnox.com

 @CarrieAnnKnox

 @CarrieAnnAuthor

 @CarrieAnnBooks